THE HIGHLANDER'S HIDDEN HEART

THE HIGHLANDER'S HIDDEN HEART

VETERANS CLUB #3

JULIE COULTER BELLON

STONE
HALL
BOOKS

Other Books by Julie Coulter Bellon

Regency

The Marquess Meets His Match

The Viscount's Vow

Canadian Spies Series

Through Love's Trials

On the Edge

Time Will Tell

Doctors and Dangers Series

All's Fair

Dangerous Connections

Ribbon of Darkness

Hostage Negotiation Series

All Fall Down (Hostage Negotiation #1)

Falling Slowly (Hostage Negotiation #1.5)

Ashes Ashes (Hostage Negotiation #2)

From the Ashes (Hostage Negotiation #2.5)

Pocket Full of Posies (Hostage Negotiation #3)

Forget Me Not (Hostage Negotiation #3.5)

Ring Around the Rosie (Hostage Negotiation #4)

Griffin Force Series

The Captive

The Captain

The Capture

Second Look

Lincoln Love Stories

Love's Broken Road

Love's Journey Home

Copyright © 2020 by Julie Coulter Bellon.

Published by Stone Hall Books

Cover Design by Steven Novak Illustrations

ISBN 13: 978-0-9997946-9-2

Printed in the United States of America

10 9 8 7 6 5 4 3 2 1

ACKNOWLEDGMENTS

I am so grateful to all the people who have helped me get this book ready. Jon, Jeni, and Jodi, my three "J"s are always up for a last-minute read or to help me make the story stronger. Thank you!

Annette, my critique partner, is one of my biggest cheerleaders and is always sure this is my best story yet. Thank you!

As always, my SWAT team is amazing and I am so grateful for all their help.

And to my family—thank you for being so patient as I tried to juggle so many things these past months. I am so humbled and grateful for all of your words of encouragement and support as I follow my dreams. I love you!

For all those who feel like they don't fit in—never give up on love.

CHAPTER 1

*A*lec Ramsay looked out the carriage window, trying to hide his dismay. London was crowded, dirty, and he already felt restricted with his cravat and waistcoat, attire befitting a new English earl. If he could have gotten away with traveling in a comfortable kilt, he would have. But his mother had insisted he try to fit in as a new peer of England. This was his chance to have land of his own and a legacy to pass down to his children, she'd said, and he shouldn't waste the opportunity. So he'd obliged her and put the kilt in his trunks. He'd been regretting that decision for miles.

He pulled the curtain closed and turned to look at his mother sitting across from him. Isabella Ramsay was a beautiful woman, her jet-black hair and striking green eyes matching his own, evidence of their proud Scottish heritage. She had the heart of a warrior, and he'd seen her fierceness many times. Today, in the heart of London, however, he could sense her nervousness. She was stroking her dog Kitty's long, silky hair, both of them, it seemed, needing the comforting motion.

"Are ye tired, Ma?" he asked.

Both his mother and Kitty looked over at him as if they had intentionally synchronized their actions. "Kitty needs to go for a walk soon." She adjusted the Skye terrier's weight on her lap. "And now that we're in London, you need to remember to use proper English and not sound like a Scot. That could smooth your way into society's good graces."

Alec barely refrained from rolling his eyes. That chastisement had become a repetitive reminder ever since they'd left home. She wanted so badly for him to fit in among the English, as if he hadn't been raised on Campbell lands. He was a Highlander, and such a heritage wasn't easily thrust aside by a missive naming him the new Earl of Suffield.

He sat back against the squabs, wishing he'd never seen the document from the solicitor. The chances of him inheriting the title had been so slim, he'd never given it a thought, but here they were in London with the old earl and both of his sons deceased and Alec named as heir. All the plans he'd had for his life had turned upside down. And now he'd removed to London, where people wore uncomfortable clothes, and, apparently, were always proper in behavior and speech as well.

Alec breathed a sigh of relief as they finally pulled up to Suffield House. He didn't wait for the coachman to put out the step and instead opened the carriage door and hopped down himself. His mother gave him a reproving stare as she reached for his outstretched hand. "Alec."

"Yes, Ma." He helped her to the ground, careful not to jostle Kitty. The dog was a terror to anyone but his mother, and even now, her little doggy eyes stared at him balefully. Isabella bent her head and crooned in Kitty's ear that she was the very best of dogs, but the animal was obviously still displeased at their long carriage ride. She didn't look back at either of them as she

2

jumped out of Isabella's arms and ran down the crowded walkway.

"Oh!" His mother's startled gasp of alarm propelled him to action.

"Wait here," he instructed, the image of his mother wading into the crowd of people in his mind's eye. He didn't want to lose her in a strange city just as they'd arrived. "I'll get her for you."

Alec strode after the little devil dog, but she definitely had the advantage, her four legs pumping as fast as they could go as she ran away from him. With so many people strolling down the street his view of the dog was obscured momentarily, so he craned his neck to try and catch sight of her again.

"Kitty, come here," he called, spying a little flash of fur just ahead. The terrier ignored him and kept running—right into the street. Alec's heart skipped a beat as a carriage swerved out of the way, narrowly missing the little dog.

"Kitty," he yelled to the frightened animal, hoping she would come to his voice, or at least come away from the busy road. She did, zigzagging back to the walk and barreling toward a young woman with her maid. Both women were wide-eyed, watching the dog drama unfold.

The lady crouched and held out her arms. She seemed unconcerned about her pretty yellow gown being soiled, her entire attention on the frightened dog. Kitty must have sensed as much, for she fairly leaped into the stranger's arms.

"Oh, you p-poor thing. Are you all right?" she cooed, pulling her close. Kitty, visibly trembling, licked the woman's hand. "You're a s-sweet girl," she said with a smile.

Quickly catching up to the pair, Alec reached out his hand to help the woman to her feet. "Thank ye, lass," he said as she straightened. "My ma would be heartbroken if anything happened to her wee dog."

As if his words had conjured her, his mother appeared at his side. "Kitty," she said, her hand at her throat. "You naughty girl. Come to Mama." She reached out for her pet.

With one last squeeze, the young woman in yellow surrendered Kitty. His mother cuddled the dog close, but kept her eyes on Kitty's rescuer. Her maid was brushing out her lady's skirts and eyeing Kitty suspiciously, as if she might jump for her mistress again.

"She really is a good little thing," Alec's mother explained. "But she's been cooped up in a carriage for too long, I'm afraid, and wanted to stretch her legs. It's all my fault, really. I was anxious to reach London."

The woman swallowed visibly before speaking. "She's a b-beautiful dog, and I'm g-glad she wasn't hurt. Did you say her n-name is *Kitty*?" The young woman spoke slowly and carefully, as she looked between Alec and Isabella.

"Yes, it's Kitty." Alec gave his mother a warm glance. "If I'd ever had a sister, that would have been her name."

"It's a fine name." Isabella drew her lips down into a little *moue* at Alec's explanation. "And it suits her." She gave Kitty a kiss, as if soothing the dog's feelings at the insult.

"I-I agree. A f-fine name." The woman's blue eyes turned to Alec, filled with laughter and merriment as she suppressed a smile. She stepped closer, and Alec's breath caught. She was the epitome of a fine English lass, with fair, creamy skin, and honey-blonde hair, but that sparkle to her eyes was unexpected and drew him in. She seemed familiar somehow, but they'd never met before. He would have surely remembered meeting her.

His mother nudged his arm, and he realized he'd been staring. He bowed, trying to recover from his blunder.

"Well, thank you for helping me retrieve her," Alec said, a rueful grin on his face. "'Twas very kind of you. It's been a long day of travel, and I suppose we need to settle in."

"Come, my lady," the maid put in, as if relieved to finally be saying goodbye to the dog and her owner. "We shouldn't tarry in the street."

The young woman nodded but seemed reluctant to go. She put her hand to the brim of her fashionable bonnet, looking down the street where Alec and Isabella's carriage still stood next to Suffield House.

"Are you r-relatives of Lord Suffield?" she asked, before a flush crept up her neck and a crease of worry appeared on her forehead. "I'm s-sorry. That's an impertinent question, and my mother would be m-mortified to know I'd said it aloud."

Her deliberate speech had a melodic cadence that was hypnotizing, and Alec was falling under its spell. More importantly, though, he recognized a kindred spirit in her since Alec often mortified his own mother.

"I won't tell her if you won't." He smiled in reassurance and tilted his head toward the young woman. "If I may introduce us, this is my mother, Lady Isabella Ramsay, and I'm Alec Ramsay, the new Earl of Suffield. We've just arrived in town."

Isabella nudged him again, her elbow sharp in his side. "It isn't proper to introduce yourself," she said under her breath.

"Whyever not?" Alec asked, drawing his eyebrows down. "Who else better to make the introduction than myself?"

The young woman seemed amused as she looked between them again. "Your m-mother's right." She leaned in slightly, clasping her hands in front of her. "A m-mutual acquaintance must m-make you known to me."

Alec was entranced by the smile on her lips, as if it held a wealth of secrets he would enjoy finding out. "I'm deeply sorry, then, for I don't know anyone in London yet."

The young lady held out her hand, as if expecting Alec to take it. He glanced at his mother, who seemed as perplexed as he. With a half-shrug, he took the lady's hand in his and raised an eyebrow in her direction.

"We d-do, of course, have one m-mutual acquaintance." She nodded toward the dog. "Miss Kitty, would you be so g-good as to introduce me to your friends?" Kitty tipped her head as if she understood and sniffed. "Ah yes, th-thank you, Miss Kitty. I'm so pleased to meet you b-both. I'm Lady Elizabeth B-Barrington."

"The pleasure is mine, Lady Elizabeth." Alec bent over her hand and lightly pressed a kiss to the back of her glove.

He held her fingers a moment longer than necessary, and her cheeks pinked prettily before she pulled away. "L-Lord Suffield," she murmured.

Alec wanted the moment to last, but Lady Elizabeth's maid stepped closer. "We really must be going, my lady," she said, touching her mistress's elbow. "You're late for tea."

Lady Elizabeth nodded at the maid. "Yes, of c-course." She turned her attention back to Alec and his mother. "Th-Thank you again for the introduction, M-Miss Kitty," she said with one more pat for the dog. "I'm so g-glad you weren't hurt."

She turned and walked toward the townhouse behind them, her maid in tow. Alec watched her for a moment, before Kitty's whine brought him back to the present. "Well, that was most unexpected," he murmured as he and his mother walked back to Suffield House.

"What do you make of Lady Elizabeth?" she asked, cutting him a sly glance.

"She's everything an English miss should be," he said, hiding a smile. His mother couldn't resist any opportunity to point out a bonny lass. She wanted to see him married and settled, but those were the last things on his mind since becoming an earl. He more than likely wouldn't have time for anything other than learning how to be a titled peer of the realm. If he did find time for other pursuits, however, Lady Elizabeth would be high on his list of people he wanted to know better.

"She obviously loves dogs," his mother observed. "Kitty doesn't take to just anyone, you know."

"Yes, I know," Alec said, looking down at the dog. She sniffed, as if she couldn't deign to even look at Alec. "I was going to scold her for running away, but it did lead to a new acquaintance with our neighbor, so I suppose she may be forgiven."

His mother put her free arm through his. "I hope you will make many acquaintances here." She glanced back at the carriage they'd brought from Scotland, and a tiny shadow of longing flickered over her face, but she covered it up quickly. "Now that England is our home and you have lands and tenants here, we must make the effort to be amiable and all that is expected of someone holding your title."

He patted her hand. "I know it's important to ye, Ma. But I hope ye don't have your heart set on my escort to nightly balls and parties. I'll have so many business matters to attend to that my time will be limited."

"We'll make time," she assured him. "It's important for you to make a good impression."

"A good impression?" he asked as they climbed the steps to Suffield House. "I can't think of anyone in London whose opinion is important to me." His conscience pricked him with the thought of a certain young lady of recent acquaintance. He found himself wanting her good opinion, though they'd only just met.

"I thought that too, once, when your father and I first married," his mother said softly. "But the good will of your peers will be very important. Being on the outside is a very lonely place to be."

Alec stopped at her melancholy tones and turned his mother by the shoulders to face him. "I won't have you upsetting yourself. I know you had a difficult time when you were in London as a young wife with my da, but times have changed."

"The wagging tongues never change. And they can damage you with a whisper of rumor." She adjusted Kitty in her arms. "I want better for you."

He smiled and put an arm around her. "Och, dinna fash yerself. Ye've convinced me. I'll do my best to make a good impression. For you."

She stood on her tiptoes and kissed his cheek. "You've always been a good son," she told him as they approached the front door.

Alec brushed off the front of his coat and tried to smooth his long, black hair back into his queue. His mother handed him his hat and he put it on. "Hopefully we're presentable enough after Kitty's escape attempt and a week's worth of travel."

His mother took a deep breath and looked askance at the door to the previous earl's home. She bit her lip. "I hope so, too."

The nervousness was so unlike his mother that it took Alec aback. What the devil had happened in the past to warrant such a reaction? His mother had spoken only in generalities of her time in London when she was first married, but seeing her anxiety made him want to question her further. Of course, now wasn't the time, but he vowed to find out more.

As they approached the door, a butler opened it and bowed. "Lady Isabella, Lord Suffield. Welcome to Suffield House. My name is Banks."

"Banks." Alec nodded to the older gentleman, whose salt-and-pepper hair and nearly perfect posture put Alec in mind of a retired military man. Banks was adept at his duties, and helped his mother, and then Alec, with their gloves, hats, and traveling cloaks, before ushering them into a beautiful blue and gold parlor.

"Mrs. Jennings, the housekeeper, will be bringing a small

repast," Banks told them. "We weren't exactly sure when you would arrive, but as soon as we saw the carriage, Mrs. Jennings went immediately to the kitchen to speak to Cook."

As if on cue, the housekeeper arrived with a selection of cold meat and cheeses. "Ah, Mrs. Jennings," Banks said. "There you are."

The tall, thin woman wearing a gray gown and a spotless white apron curtsied to Alec and Isabella. "Your lordship, my lady. Welcome to Suffield House."

Alec dipped his head in acknowledgment. "Thank you, Mrs. Jennings." He made sure his mother was seated comfortably with a plate in hand before he approached Banks. "Have the solicitors said when they will call?"

Banks shook his head, clasping his hands behind his back. "They are waiting for word from you, my lord."

Alec started to run his hand through his hair, but, after a pointed look from his mother, settled for rubbing his palm over the stubble on his jaw. He might as well get the solicitors' meeting taken care of as soon as possible. "Please send them a message to meet me here first thing in the morning."

Banks dipped his head. "Very good, my lord." He resumed his position near the door.

Mrs. Jennings stepped forward and smoothed down her apron before speaking. "Your rooms are aired and ready, my lord, if you and your mother would like to freshen up after your trip."

"I'm sure my mother will appreciate your attention to her care." Alec hesitated. Both servants looked at him expectantly, like schoolchildren waiting to be dismissed. "That will be all, then." The words rolled off Alec's tongue, but felt strange in his mouth. The servants at home in Scotland were more like family, with hardly any formality between them. Obviously the same could not be said in England, though they'd only just arrived. Perhaps they still could find that rapport with the servants here.

The housekeeper and butler nodded and backed out of the room, closing the door behind them. Alec joined his mother on the settee and picked up a plate, the blue edging on the china reminding him of the blue eyes of Lady Elizabeth. She'd definitely been a bright spot in a dreary day.

He took a bite of cheese, contemplating the duties he'd be expected to perform while in London. With Lady Elizabeth's smile in his mind's eye, he decided that maybe his mother was right. Taking part in society events might be just the thing to balance the tedious chores of the earldom.

At least one thing was certain—attempting to further the acquaintance of his beautiful, blue-eyed neighbor would be more diverting than anything else he'd find to entertain himself while in London.

And he was quite looking forward to it.

CHAPTER 2

*E*lizabeth ran a palm down her skirts as she stood in the hall outside her father's study. He rarely called for her, and the moments she was in his company tended to be . . . difficult. What could he possibly want with her?

She forced herself to raise her hand and knock. From an early age, she'd been taught that she wasn't allowed in her father's study without express permission, so she waited to turn the doorknob until after she'd heard her father say, "Enter."

She made the short walk to the front of her father's desk, but he hadn't yet acknowledged her presence. He signed a document and blotted it before he looked at her.

"No need for you to speak." Her father waved his hand, as if it were obvious her voice was too tedious to be borne. "This interview won't be long. I've called you here to inform you that I've accepted a suitor on your behalf. After two Seasons, it's time to see you settled."

Elizabeth put a hand to her throat, words tumbling over themselves in her mind. "Wh-Who?" she managed to croak, cursing her stutter. If she'd been able to speak to gentlemen properly, maybe she would have had more marriage offers to make her father proud and even a husband she could love someday.

"Lord Lindley." He kept his eyes on her as he spoke, and Elizabeth could hardly hide her cringe. It was well known that Lord Lindley was too full of himself by half and unkind to those he considered beneath him.

Her father must have sensed her distress, because he gentled his tone somewhat. "Before we sign any contracts, I've instructed him to court you until we make our way to Cranbourne for the holidays. That will give you time to become better acquainted."

Elizabeth shook her head. She didn't want to better acquaint herself with Lord Lindley. "N-No, Father. Please. N-Not him." Tears pricked the back of her throat. She willed them away. Her father hated tears almost as much as he hated her stutter.

The moment she spoke with her cursed stutter, any gentleness in her father disappeared. "It's for the best, you'll see." He turned his attention to the papers on his desk, effectively dismissing her.

Elizabeth stood there, frozen, wanting to refuse, to plead, to beg for more time. But words were hard for her under the best of circumstances. Though, even if she'd had a silk tongue, her father might not be swayed. When he made a decision, he rarely revisited it. Her only choice was to silently accept her fate.

As her father had known she would.

Turning on her heel, she went to her chambers to retrieve her sketchbook and then slipped outside to the garden. The late autumn weather was perfect for being outdoors, and the soft sweep of the pencil had always soothed her and helped order her thoughts. She needed that boon more than ever today.

After she'd met the new Lord Suffield two days ago, she'd been unable to get him out of her mind and had turned to sketching him. She looked down at her not-quite-finished drawing of his face, one of his best features being his kind and appreciative eyes. They had a sincerity in their depths she'd not seen in the eyes of her family or the members of the *ton* very often, if at all. Conversing so easily with the earl and his mother that day had been a surprise. Neither of them had noticed her stutter—or hadn't remarked on it if they had.

Maybe I should have visited Scotland sooner, she mused, *if the earl is an example of what that country has to offer.*

As a child, she'd had a nanny from Scotland who'd sung Scottish lullabies and soothed her fits of anger when she couldn't speak as she wished. Mary had been the one person in the world who'd loved her in spite of any shortcomings. It was Mary's voice that had encouraged her to try again, to be brave, and to not give up. Elizabeth's soul had held those words close, especially if her father was near. He didn't have patience for a daughter who couldn't get her words out right away.

But the time for Elizabeth to leave the nursery and enter the schoolroom had come far too soon. Her beloved Mary had been sent away, replaced with a stern English governess who loved to rap Elizabeth's knuckles every time she stuttered. The pain gave Elizabeth more reason than ever to stay silent. There had been no more comforting Scottish lullabies to soothe the hurts away. Until Alec had spoken and called her *lass*, she hadn't realized how much she'd missed that lilting brogue.

Privately, she allowed herself to call him Alec. Of course, she couldn't say his name aloud while in company. She was expected to comport herself in a manner above reproach, and since Elizabeth had been such a disappointment to her parents in every other way, she worked hard at remembering her manners at all times.

Though propriety had called for her to hurry inside for tea, Elizabeth had stood near the street and hugged a strange dog who'd narrowly missed being crushed by a carriage. Holding a trembling animal in her arms after such an experience had made the spontaneous meeting with the new earl much more memorable.

She sat on her favorite bench near the rosebushes. The scent of roses still clung to the little garden spot, as if reluctant to let the lovely summer aroma give way to cold weather quite yet. Elizabeth bent over her drawing, trying to get Alec's eyes just right, with his unfashionably long hair framing his face and falling to his shoulders. He'd reminded her of the panther she'd seen at the Royal Menagerie—sleek and graceful, with a hint of leashed strength in his movements.

She had an aptitude for drawing animals and portraits, so she'd started incorporating both techniques by putting features of friends, family, and *ton* members into an animal of Elizabeth's choosing. She'd drawn her best friend, Alice, as a lioness, beautiful and proud, willing to defend her loved ones at any cost. Her father's animal portrait was a ram, small of stature, but with a ducal air of authority, hinting that he'd use his horns to butt heads with anyone who stood in his way.

After the Earl of Lindley had started to pay his addresses at the two social events she'd forced herself to endure the past few weeks, she'd drawn him as a fish, his trademark high forehead far above the smaller fish swimming with him in the pond. His pompous air was reflected in the drawing, as were his slimy lips, which always gave a little smack over her glove whenever he kissed her hand in greeting.

Most of her past portraits had a fanciful air to them, but today, she'd put them aside for a pair of Scottish eyes that had drawn her focus, and the memories of how he'd lingered over her hand. Her cheeks heated again at the remembrance. She'd never before wished for more time to converse with a gentleman, but with Alec, her words had finally flowed. The feeling had been so new and wonderful, she hadn't wanted to leave.

"Best not let her ladyship see that one," Tess, her maid, said, appearing over her shoulder. "She'd have a fit of the vapors for certain."

Elizabeth stifled a startled gasp and put a hand to her chest. "You f-frightened me, Tess."

"That earl was too friendly by far. And keeping a lady standing in the street!" The maid clucked. "He needs some lessons in manners."

"I found him q-quite amiable." *And handsome*, Elizabeth added silently. But she didn't want to discuss Alec with anyone, so she quickly turned the pages back to her fish drawing of Lindley. The warmth from earlier dissipated as she eyed the portrait critically. "I th-think his eyebrows are a bit too b-bushy for a fish."

Tess took the sketchbook from her and held it up. "Perhaps, but the forehead is quite realistic. It must be cumbersome to have such a prominent feature."

"The easier to l-look down on p-people." Elizabeth's shoulders slumped at the thought of him as her husband. "All of my ch-children may very well have that f-forehead." She set aside her sketchbook. "My father has given him leave to c-court me until w-we repair to Cranbourne." She shivered. Elizabeth wished they were already on their way there. At least at her family's country seat, she wasn't expected to constantly converse with new acquaintances.

Tess watched her closely, taking a moment before she spoke. "Your father merely wants you settled, my lady."

"And I will be s-settling—s-settling for a husband who is over-b-bearing and unkind." Her voice sounded bitter to her own ears, but she couldn't help it.

"You'll never want for anything, my lady. And you'll have children to love," Tess pointed out, bending to pick up the pencils beside Elizabeth on the stone bench. "But if we're going to have you looking your best for the Huntingdon ball this evening, we'd best go in. Your mother said the coach won't wait for you."

Elizabeth didn't want to go out. She never did. Balls were a chore and always had been. When she was nervous, her stutter grew worse, and she hated the resulting whispers and stares. But the Huntingdon ball was the one event she couldn't miss out of respect for Alice and her parents. She closed her sketchbook and stood. "I suppose we m-must, then."

"The Duke and Duchess of Huntingdon always throw wonderful balls, my lady. And though Alice hasn't returned from the country yet, it might be diverting," Tess said brightly, obviously trying to think of something cheering to say as the two women started for the house.

"I can't wait for Alice to come home," Elizabeth said, knowing Alice's absence at her mother and father's ball would leave a void too large to be filled. "I hope she's having a wonderful time with her marquess." It was still strange to think of Alice as a married woman. She'd had such a whirlwind courtship that only family had attended the actual ceremony, so the marriage didn't seem quite real yet. Elizabeth was anxious to meet Alice's new husband, the Marquess of Wolverton.

"The letters you've mentioned from the new marchioness seem full of happy news," Tess said as they approached the side entrance to the house.

"Yes, they do." Alice had made a love match, and Elizabeth envied her that now. They'd always dreamed of dashing heroes who would carry them off, but Lindley wasn't the sort to carry anything but a grudge. Elizabeth sighed. Being so morose wouldn't do, but her future as the Countess of Lindley yawned before her in all its dreary glory.

Clutching her sketchbook tighter to her side, she thought of the eyes she'd painstakingly drawn—Alec's eyes. Perhaps he'd be at the ball this evening. The thought put a little spring in her step and a smile on her face. Maybe there would be a reason to look her best tonight after all.

"Come along, Tess. There is much to do."

Tess seemed to sense her change in mood and hurried to keep pace with her. "Yes, my lady."

After hours of primping and dressing, then having her hair curled and piled high on her head with a few strategic curls to frame her face, Elizabeth barely made it to the coach on time. Her mother didn't comment, merely motioned for the coach to drive on. Elizabeth's feelings were all a-muddle, however. Dread filled her, knowing Lindley would be in attendance and view her as his future wife. But there was also a tingle of anticipation at the possibility of seeing Alec again. Surely a new earl would be invited to the Huntingdon ball.

If he was there, would she be able to speak to him again? Would he ask her to dance? She held a hand to her middle to calm herself. Her mother had lectured her long and often about a lady having an air of tranquility, but Elizabeth would have to dig deep to find the strength for that quality tonight.

They walked into the great hall overflowing with hothouse roses and lit with so many candles, the room was as light as noonday. They moved through the receiving line, where her mother greeted their hosts and stepped forward so Elizabeth could as well. The Duke and Duchess of Huntingdon were old family friends—their daughter, Alice, was the only friend Elizabeth had in the world—so as Elizabeth rose from her curtsy, she wasn't surprised to see the duchess wink at her.

"Lady Elizabeth," the duchess said, taking her arm. "With my Alice still in the country for another week, I've taken it upon myself to introduce you to a fellow animal lover." With a glance at her mother for permission, Elizabeth let herself be led away from the reception line in the front hall toward the ballroom. "They've only just arrived in town, and when I met them earlier this afternoon, I knew you had to make their acquaintance."

The duchess knew of Elizabeth's shyness and inability to speak to gentlemen, so this new acquaintance must be a woman. The thought calmed her nerves. Elizabeth tried to hide her amusement at the duchess's excitement. "I d-don't believe I've seen you this enthusiastic in ages, Your G-Grace."

She squeezed Elizabeth's arm. "You're like my own daughter, and I wish you'd call me Dorothy." The older woman smiled and leaned closer. "I've watched you these past weeks since Alice left, dear girl, and you seem in need of a diversion. The twinkle in your eyes has dimmed."

How easily she saw Elizabeth's emotions while her own mother didn't. "D-Dorothy," she murmured. "You are too k-kind."

A man and a woman stood in the corner of the ballroom, their heads bent close together. Her eyes widened when she recognized Alec and his mother. The few butterflies she'd had in her middle earlier suddenly returned in droves. As if he felt the pull as well, Alec raised his head, his green eyes focused solely on her, making her feel as if she were the only lady in the room. She couldn't help the color that rose to her cheeks.

The Duchess of Huntingdon inclined her head toward Alec's mother. "Lady Isabella, I'd like to make known to you Lady Elizabeth, daughter of the Duke of Barrington."

Lady Isabella curtsied. "I'm pleased to make your acquaintance." Her eyes lit with amusement at this second introduction. "And may I make known to you my son, the Earl of Suffield."

The earl bowed over the duchess's hand, and then Elizabeth's. He kissed the back of her glove once again, and she could hardly suppress her smile. She felt a blush suffuse her face, the heat going all the way to the tips of her ears, as his grip on her fingers tightened for just a moment before he released her.

"My mother and I were so grateful for your visit and kind invitation to tonight's festivities, Your Grace," Alec said, turning his focus to the older woman. "We sorely needed a night out in company."

He was speaking slowly, trying to mask his Scottish accent, and Elizabeth felt a feeling of camaraderie go through her. That's exactly how she tried to hide her stutter. But why was he changing his speech? To make a good impression? Some still looked down on Scots, she supposed.

The Duchess of Huntingdon gave Alec a smile. "I was dear friends with your grandmother, the Countess of Suffield, so I must include you both among my friends as well." She turned to Isabella. "I was just telling Lady Elizabeth about your delightful dog, Kitty. She's a Skye terrier, is she not?"

"Yes," Isabella replied, relaxing a little in the face of the duchess's friendliness. "Quite a popular breed where we're from. She was a gift from my father."

"I've long wanted a Skye terrier of my own," the duchess confided. "I've yet to see one with such fine hair and temperament as yours. Since Lady Elizabeth adores dogs, I knew she must make your acquaintance at once."

Elizabeth held her gloved hand to her lips as her eyes met Alec's. Kitty's "fine temperament" had not been on display the day they'd met, as she'd nearly bowled Elizabeth over running amok in the street.

"Do you own a dog, then, my lady?" Alec asked with a straight face, yet his eyes clearly showed amusement at their shared observation.

Elizabeth swallowed, hoping her stutter wouldn't be too obvious. "I h-have a hound dog named George," she told him, pleased her words were clear. She didn't feel so nervous when Alec's smile was directed at her. "He's quite old and spends most of his t-time by the fire or in the k-kitchen."

She couldn't remember a time when George hadn't been part of the household. He was the one who held all her girlish secrets and protected her by chasing all the ghastly birds away during their rambles in the woods.

"Yes, warmth and food are very important to dogs," he said, chuckling. "Kitty's life is much the same as George's, except she spends her time in my mother's chambers or near her elbow, waiting for a biscuit."

His mother and Dorothy smiled and nodded to each other, but Elizabeth kept her eyes on Alec. He was dressed in black except for his blue and silver waistcoat and white cravat. His hair was freshly trimmed and had been combed into submission. He looked every inch the English gentleman and cut quite the dashing figure.

Oh, how she wished Alice were here to talk to!

Alec tilted his head, aware of her perusal, and Elizabeth felt another flush creeping up her cheeks. How gauche to be caught staring, but she couldn't look away.

"As the musicians are striking up a country dance I am familiar with, may I ask you to dance, my lady?" Alec asked. "Then we can exchange more stories about our family pets."

The eyes of those in their circle turned to her, and Elizabeth hoped her face wasn't as red as it felt.

"Of c-course." A little thrill shot through her as he held out his arm to escort her to the floor. His arm was solid and steady under her hand. She resisted the urge to tighten her grip and draw closer to him. What was it about this man that made propriety seem unimportant? Lately, she could think of nothing else but being near him.

It seemed as if all eyes were upon them as they took their

positions. Everyone who attended society events knew she didn't dance often. Elizabeth was more likely to be found among the chaperones or hidden in a corner, trying to be as invisible as possible. Their judgmental stares always made her self-conscious, and she usually tensed when the musicians began to play, but this time, with Alec's smile and confident grip on her arm, she relaxed.

"The English country dance is similar to a Scottish one," he confided. "I was worried I'd be a wallflower the entire evening."

She pressed her lips into a line to suppress her laugh. The thought of this tall, handsome Scot being overlooked or relegated to a corner was ridiculous. "I understand the s-sentiment," she said gravely. "B-Being a wallflower can be a t-terrible blow when you love to d-dance."

They separated for a moment before they could speak again. "I'm sure you dinna have that problem," he said with an appreciative gleam in his eye. "English lords would have to be dunderheids otherwise."

His Scottish brogue was coming out again. Elizabeth felt warmth wash over her as it had at their first meeting. Something about the way he spoke when he was comfortable immediately put her at ease.

"How is K-Kitty?" Elizabeth asked as she came close. "R-Recovered from her adventure?" The words had never slipped so easily from her lips with any other gentleman, and it was exhilarating. She had worried so often that carrying on a conversation while dancing was beyond her capabilities, but it was happening.

"Aye, she's recovered," he said, looking down at her before they separated for another turn. "And hopefully she's learned her lesson about running away."

Elizabeth caught sight of Lindley watching her from the edge of the dance floor, a scowl on his face. Holding back a sigh, she turned under Alec's arm, wishing the dance would never end. "Sometimes I wish I could r-run away," she murmured.

Alec followed her gaze. "Is he bothering ye, lass?"

The concern in his voice, combined with the way he called her *lass*, trickled over her senses like the warm chocolate she drank every morning. A frisson of heat blazed a trail all the way to her toes as she regarded the man in front of her.

"N-No, my lord," she said, as he carefully twirled her around him in the final steps of the dance. "I j-just understand how Kitty f-feels. I am w-watched over carefully, but there are t-times when I'd like to b-break free."

The music stopped, but he gazed into her eyes for an extra moment before escorting her off the floor. As they maneuvered through the crowd, Alec bent close to her ear, and a little shiver went through her at his nearness. "I know a bit about wanting to taste freedom and choose yer own path. If ye ever have need of a friend to listen or to stand with ye, well, I'm here."

Elizabeth's heart skipped a beat at his words. He was offering friendship, even an alliance of a sort. She smiled up at him, a lump in her throat at the sweet gesture. "Th-Thank you. I won't forget."

When they drew close to the Duchess of Huntingdon, Elizabeth could see her mother standing next to Dorothy. Her fan was fluttering furiously, which had always been a signal to Elizabeth that her mother was not pleased and holding her irritation inside. What could be wrong?

"M-Mother," Elizabeth said, anxious to soothe whatever was worrying her. In her haste, Elizabeth's tongue tripped over itself. "I'd l-l-like to introduce you to the Earl of S-S-Suffield."

Alec acted as if there was nothing amiss and bowed low. "Your Grace, I'm pleased to make your acquaintance."

The careful speech was back, the proper English earl in fine form. Elizabeth decided to follow his lead. If she took the time to calm herself and think about what she wanted to say, it was easier to speak clearly and slowly. Her stutter wasn't as noticeable.

Her mother frowned slightly in Elizabeth's direction before she regally inclined her head in acknowledgment and spoke to Alec. "I understand you have a beautiful dog. Her Grace can't stop talking about her."

Elizabeth breathed a sigh of relief, grateful that Kitty was smoothing the way for yet another conversation tonight.

The Duchess of Huntingdon's hand hovered near her throat. "You would love her, too, if you could see her," she declared. "I'm going to talk to my husband about finding a dog for me."

Elizabeth's gaze slid over to Alec, but he was looking at someone behind her, a frown creasing his forehead. She didn't have to wait long to see who it was. The Earl of Lindley appeared at her elbow.

"My lady," he said a touch too loudly before bowing over her hand. His lips made their familiar smacking sound, and Elizabeth nearly cringed. "You were spirited away before I could claim you for a dance. Perhaps I might have this one?"

"Of c-course, my l-lord," Elizabeth murmured. A quick glance at the fan in her mother's hand slowing down to a leisurely pace showed how pleased the duchess was at her acceptance of Lindley's request, but Elizabeth's stomach tightened. This was the man her parents had chosen for her to marry, but all she felt when she looked at him was distaste. As she let him lead her to the dance floor, she could feel Alec's eyes on her. If only she were dancing with him again.

The music began and Elizabeth curtsied to her partner, but as she rose, Lindley leaned his head close enough to hers that she could smell his hair pomade. "I was not pleased to be forced to watch my future bride dancing with a filthy Scot," he hissed, throwing a look over his shoulder where Alec still watched them.

"My sources tell me he's not only a Scot, but a savage Highlander."

Elizabeth thought back to Alec's kind eyes and their shared laughter. "H-He's an English earl, my l-lord. And I haven't seen any savage b-behavior at all." From Alec, at least. The idea of Alec as a savage was too ridiculous for words, but whispers and rumors among the *ton* could be vicious if left unchecked. Her protective instincts rose. "He's c-carried himself w-well and is all that is p-proper," she added.

"We'll see how long that lasts," he murmured, glancing at Alec one more time.

Elizabeth's heart sank. Alec was obviously trying hard to take his place among the *ton*. If the opportunity arose when she could use whatever influence she had to help smooth the way for him, she would take it.

After all, he'd offered to stand beside her as a friend, and it seemed only right that she do the same.

CHAPTER 3

*A*lec's head was starting to ache, and it wasn't even luncheon yet. His solicitor, Mr. Lloyd, had presented himself at the townhouse early that morning to go over yet more estate business. Alec had already signed over a dozen documents and still had quite a large pile to finish. Before he signed anything else or heard more of Mr. Lloyd's accounting of estate assets, however, he got up from his desk and tugged on the bell pull.

Banks quickly appeared. "Yes, my lord?"

"Please bring a tea tray for both me and Mr. Lloyd." He needed sustenance and the solicitor probably did, too.

Banks bowed. "Right away, my lord."

Once Banks had gone for the tea tray, Alec sat down behind his desk and faced Mr. Lloyd again. "Forgive the interruption. So what you're saying is that my grandfather and my Uncle John were careful men, who did well with the earldom's assets and we are in fine financial form."

"Yes, my lord. Most of their fortune was put toward improving the lands and holdings. The tenants seem happy and productive.

Oh, and the earl had also recently bought a thoroughbred named Ares. He planned to breed racehorses, I believe." The man pushed his glasses up his rather long nose as he perused the parchment in his hand.

Alec straightened. "A thoroughbred?"

"Yes, my lord. Currently stabled at . . ." He tapped the parchment. "Oh, yes, here it is, the horse is at Lanford Park."

Excitement curled through Alec's belly. He'd started a horse breeding venture in Scotland with his Uncle Colin. The endeavor had just started to bear fruit when Alec had been called to England. Perhaps Colin could partner with him using the English thoroughbred with their best-bred horse from Scotland. The first moment he could spare, he wanted to ride out and inspect Ares. Bless his old grandpapa for his foresight.

Mr. Lloyd ate heartily from the tea tray that Banks brought for them. Alec particularly enjoyed Cook's scones and jams. He didn't have any trouble signing the last of the papers and seeing Mr. Lloyd out. Perhaps with the solicitor's meeting now attended to, Alec could take a jaunt down to Lanford Park today and then write to Colin about his findings. There was no one in the realm who knew more about horses than Colin Campbell. Perhaps he would even convince his uncle to travel to England if a thoroughbred was involved.

He returned to his study and sat down in the worn leather chair behind his desk. The furniture in the townhouse was mostly new and fashionable, but the chair the old earl must have spent a great deal of time in was well-loved and comfortable. The leather had just enough give that it was easy to sink into. If Alec was going to spend hours here tending to ledgers and meeting with stewards and solicitors, the chair was definitely a fine feature. He liked the idea that his grandfather had obviously felt the same and hadn't replaced it.

Settling in, he picked at the last scone. The golden goodness in his hand reminded him of the golden threads in Lady Elizabeth's gown she'd had on last evening. They'd made her shimmer in the candlelight and set off the sunshine blonde of her hair and the blue of her eyes. She'd looked magnificent. She was a bonny lass for certain.

He rubbed his chin. The rest of the evening had gone well, too. It hadn't been as difficult as he'd imagined to suppress his accent last night. He'd been proud of his efforts, and so had his ma. Mostly, he found that if he asked a lord about his estate, Alec didn't have to do much talking at all. The English were fond of talking about themselves and only needed a knowing nod every now and then in response to their rambling. If that's what Elizabeth had to look forward to at every society event, no wonder she wished for a bit of freedom.

He'd been surprised at her admission, which brought all of his protective instincts rushing to the fore. He'd been as proper as could be, however, and offered his friendship, nothing more. His rebellious streak had wanted to spirit her out to the terrace and offer her a wee bit of the freedom she craved. Instead, he'd handed her over to that dunderheid Lindley, who'd acted as if Elizabeth belonged to him and Alec had poached her. The man was lucky Elizabeth hadn't seemed afraid of him, merely resigned to his attentions. Surely her father wouldn't allow such a self-centered man to court his only daughter. But then, what did Alec know of an English duke's mind?

With a sigh, he pushed back from his desk. He still had to go over the ledgers and become familiar with the way the land stewards reported to him, so, though he wished he could toss everything aside and head to Lanford Park, that wouldn't be possible today. He did need a break, though, and some freedom of his own.

Maybe a ride through Hyde Park would suit. He strode to the hall and called for Banks.

"Have my horse saddled," he said to the butler. The man gave him a crisp nod, and by the time Alec had donned his coat, hat, and gloves, the horse was being led out.

As he rode toward Hyde Park, he looked around the crowded streets and thought of the wide, open spaces at Inverary Castle. His heart squeezed at the connections and family he'd left behind, but he was resolute that his future was in England. In Scotland, he was part of the Duke of Argyll's household, which was an honor, but here in England, he was an earl in his own right, with responsibilities and duties to his people and their livelihood. And truth be told, he'd always wanted to honor his father's memory in some way. Becoming the earl and doing a good job of it seemed the obvious choice.

As he entered the park, Alec was glad it wasn't as crowded as the streets behind him. The fashionable hour would probably bring out more horses, carriages, and people, but for now, only a few groups were scattered throughout the park. He let out a breath, the grass and trees comforting him in a way he couldn't explain.

Heading for Rotten Row, Alec hadn't gone far before he saw some familiar blonde curls underneath a very fashionable hat. Lady Elizabeth and her maid were on horseback, conversing with two gentlemen. For a brief moment, Alec thought about retreating so he wouldn't have to play the English gentleman today, but the opportunity to talk to Elizabeth trumped any misgivings.

He approached the small group and reined in his horse. "Good afternoon, my lady," he said, noting her stylish, deep-green riding habit. It reminded him of the color of the grass at Inverary after a rainstorm, but was even more vibrant on the woman before him. He'd yet to see any color that didn't flatter her.

"L-Lord Suffield," Elizabeth inclined her head. "T-Taking some air?"

"I have heard Scots do love to *take* things," the gentlemen near her snickered. "And I don't mean air."

Alec didn't know the man, but he recognized the Earl of Lindley on the other side of Elizabeth. Lindley leaned forward in his saddle, as if to relate a confidence to his friend, but spoke loud enough for all to hear. "It's not a wonder he needs to take air. We all might, with the crude stench that's suddenly wafted into this area." He looked pointedly in Alec's direction.

Alec's jaw tightened at the insults, and he was grateful his mother wasn't with him. Her pained admission that the *ton's* good graces were important to her was the only thing keeping him from showing both gentlemen how a "crude" Scot could "take" them off their horses for a lesson in manners.

Making a valiant attempt to concentrate on the reason he'd stopped in the first place, Alec ignored the men. "Thank you for asking, Lady Elizabeth. I find the air in London quite hot, and shall we say, blustery?" He tilted his head slightly toward Lindley, but kept his eyes on her. "I'm glad to see you about on this fine morning."

Lindley frowned as the double meaning of hot and blustery sank in, and his fists clenched around his reins. "You aren't fit to look upon Lady Elizabeth. We are all good English stock here, and a barbarian Scot does not have leave to speak to us in that manner." He sniffed and looked down his nose at Alec.

"My lord," Elizabeth said, glaring at Lindley. "That w-was uncalled for. You owe the Earl of S-Suffield an apology."

Alec knew he would never get an apology from the man. Patting his horse's neck, Alec counted to ten before he answered. "I, also, am from good English stock on my father's side. However, he had the great foresight to marry the granddaughter of the Duke of Argyll so some Scottish blood could add a little backbone to the English line."

Lindley's eyes narrowed. "Perhaps I might show you some English backbone."

Elizabeth's brows arched as she realized his meaning, the tension swirling around them getting heavier with each comment. She maneuvered her horse closer to Alec. "Lord Lindley, th-that is quite enough."

"No one asked you," Lindley snarled. "Why are you defending him?"

"She's not defending me, you dolt. She's appalled at your manners." Alec wanted to reach out to her. The shine in her eyes testified that Lindley had hurt her feelings.

"Lord S-Suffield, will you p-please escort me home?" she asked quietly.

"Of course." Alec turned his horse so they were side by side, but before they could leave, Lindley barred Elizabeth's way.

"I believe your mother is expecting *me* to return you home," he said with a frown. "After all, my suit has been accepted by your father, and I've been given leave to court you."

"You're doing a terrible job of it," Alec put in. "The lady has asked for my escort, and I intend to give it to her."

Elizabeth didn't wait for the end of the debate, but spurred her horse on, forcing Lindley out of the way. Her maid and Alec followed close behind, their horses making a soft, snorting sound as if happy to be moving again. He couldn't resist a look back at the other two men. Lindley had gotten his horse under control and watched Elizabeth with a scowl on his face. Did the man have any other expression when it came to her?

When they'd turned a corner, Lady Elizabeth slowed, unable to hide her tears. Alec came up beside her, taking a handkerchief out of his pocket to give to her.

"Don't fash yerself over a dunderheid like that," he said. Tears clung to her lashes as she took his offering and dabbed at her eyes. The sight made him want to plant a facer on that clod Lindley.

"Would you m-mind if we walked for a bit, L-Lord Suffield?" she asked softly, sniffling into the small square of cloth.

"Not at all." He dismounted and quickly came to her side. "But when we're in private, would you please call me Alec? Lord Suffield sounds so formal and strange to my ears."

"Only if y-you call me Elizabeth." She stared down at him from her perch atop the horse for a moment, bleakness shadowing her eyes. Had Lindley upset her that much?

Finally, she reached for his shoulders, and he slid his hands around her small waist. Slowly, he lifted her off the horse and settled her on the path. Her fingers squeezed his shoulders and his grip on her tightened. With her in his arms, time seemed to stop. Attraction for this wee English lass zipped through him so fast it stole his breath. She mesmerized him.

"Th-Thank you," she said, breaking the silence, her gaze locked on his. "You're so very k-kind." She held her horse's reins, but didn't seem in a hurry to go anywhere.

Alec's horse whickered behind him, as if urging him to action. He held out his elbow to her. "Shall we?"

Elizabeth looked behind her as two young men in livery approached them on horseback. Had she been required to bring two grooms with her on a mere outing to the park, as well as her maid? She seemed unsurprised at their advance and waited for them to come closer.

He watched her clasp her hands and take a deep breath before speaking. "P-Please hold the horses here."

"Yes, my lady," the older-looking of the two responded as he dismounted and reached for the reins.

Alec moved to the maid's side and helped her off the horse.

She'd hung back, not speaking, but keeping a close eye on her charge, as most maids were trained to do. The young men walked the horses a short distance away. Everything was as it should be for propriety's sake, Alec supposed. He could still see the tension in the way Elizabeth carried herself, however. How could he alleviate her distress?

Elizabeth turned to her maid, motioning toward the bench. "Tess, I n-need some time to gather m-myself. I won't walk far, b-but I'd like you to w-wait for me here."

Tess looked at Alec, then back at Elizabeth. It was easy to see she had something to say, but was warring within herself. "I can stay several feet behind you, my lady," she said finally, trying to offer an acceptable compromise.

"Please, just w-wait for me on the b-bench," Elizabeth pleaded. "G-Give me a few m-minutes of privacy."

Tess could barely contain the protest that was obviously on her mind, but she managed to bob her head. "I'll be waiting right here," she said. "But please stay within sight." This time her raised eyebrows and firm lips were a message for Alec. Though she couldn't have been much older than Elizabeth, she obviously took her responsibility to watch over her mistress seriously.

"Of c-course," Elizabeth said, a look of relief crossing her features.

Alec tied his horse's reins to a tree near the bench where Tess had agreed to wait and offered Elizabeth his arm. The resignation in her eyes made Alec even more determined to do something to cheer her. She took his arm with a gusty sigh, as if the weight of the world rested on her slender shoulders. They walked a few paces away before Alec spoke.

"Been a tryin' morning, has it?" he asked softly. The leaves in the trees were rustling, nature's own music, a lulling background for a difficult day. At least it always had been for him.

Elizabeth bent her head as if to rest it against his shoulder, and he found himself wishing she would. He wanted to support her and hear her troubles. They took several more steps before she replied. "Sometimes d-doing your d-duty doesn't feel as n-noble as one would expect."

"Though I don't know any of the details of what you are referring to, I agree." When she didn't elaborate, he decided to attempt to distract her by taking her into his confidence. "I've been feeling that all my dreams are being swallowed up by my new duties."

Her fingers tightened on his arm. "Yes, that's exactly it." She glanced up at him. "What were your d-dreams?"

"My Uncle Colin and I had hopes to breed horses for racing. We'd laid all the groundwork before I was called to England." He met her eyes. "I miss working with the horses. There's nothing like riding as if the devil's own hounds are nipping at yer heels."

She let out a low laugh. "I used to love riding with my hair flying behind me. I haven't r-ridden like that since I was a g-girl. Ladies are always supposed to be sensible and p-poised, you know." Elizabeth was trying to be light-hearted, but her faded smile gave her away. As if she knew she'd been found out, she dropped her gaze to the ground.

"Is that what's botherin' ye, then?" he asked gently.

She stopped walking and faced him. After some deep breaths, she raised her chin. "When I l-left for my ride today, I had a m-maid and two g-grooms with me, as well as a gentleman escort. When I g-go to a ball, I am watched over to m-maintain my reputation, and at n-no time am I supposed to be disagreeable, even if the gentleman is a b-bounder!" Raising her face to the sky, she closed her eyes. "There are t-times when I w-want to be alone and raise my f-fists to shout at the heavens."

Alec looked at her upturned face and could barely resist lifting his hand to skim his knuckles lightly over her cheek. Her skin looked silky soft, and he'd want to linger, so it was best if he didn't start down that path. "Aye, being smothered like that would make any person daft, but I can't abide the wish, my lady."

Her eyes snapped open, and she took a step back. "Oh, of-of course. I apologize. That was unmannerly of m-me to say something outrageous and m-make you uncomfortable."

Alec closed the small distance between them and shushed her. "*Wheest*, lass. I only meant about the being alone part. If you're going to shout to the heavens, then I want to be there with ye."

She reached for his arm, her fingers curling around his bicep. "Wouldn't w-we be a sight?" A genuine smile returned to her face, and Alec was glad to see it. "I d-didn't expect to f-find someone who m-might understand my feelings."

"Both of us are in dire need of a respite from our duties, and I have just the thing." He covered her other hand with his. Walking with her fitted against his side felt right, as if she belonged there.

"What is it?" she asked. The sparkle was creeping back into her eyes, and a feeling of satisfaction arrowed through him.

"We could spend time with Kitty and George. Dogs are the easiest way to forget your troubles." He patted her hand. "And we still haven't introduced them to each other yet."

"An egregious oversight, I'm sure." She leaned into him until their shoulders touched. "I'll s-see if George is up to c-calling on a lady."

"Or you could come to Suffield House and call on my mother. Kitty will be with her, and we can ask if she's up to receiving a gentleman caller." He wanted to show her Suffield House and use the time to further add to his knowledge of this fascinating woman beside him.

Elizabeth watched him carefully before she put some distance between them and turned back the way they'd come. "Let's ccollect Tess, then, so I can m-make a call on Miss Kitty." She looked over her shoulder at him. "If you're sure that's acceptable?"

Alec quickly caught up to her. Miss Kitty was quite temperamental when it came to guests, actually, but he wasn't about to mention that detail.

"A brilliant idea," he assured her. But the words died on his lips when he saw the Earl of Lindley stalking toward him, his face grim.

"I've come to collect my lady," he said as he drew near, leading his horse behind him. "And show you an English backbone."

Alec pulled Elizabeth closer, wanting to shield her. Lindley was obviously going to force a confrontation.

"D-Don't engage him," Elizabeth said quietly, her voice edged with anxiety as Lindley watched them, his animosity nearly palpable. "He's not known for fair fights."

"But I must engage," he said, wishing there were another way, but knowing there wasn't. "He's given me no choice."

"There's always a ch-choice," Elizabeth said. The resigned look in her eyes had returned, however. Snuffing out Elizabeth's spark twice in one day was Lindley's worst offense. For that, Alec wouldn't back down.

Lightly squeezing her shoulder to reassure her, Alec bent so she'd meet his eyes and feel his sincerity. "I apologize for the delay, lass," he said, trying to lighten the mood a bit. "But I promise I'll return shortly so we can continue with our plans to call on my mother."

Just as soon as he'd shown this Englishman how the Earl of Suffield dealt with dunderheids.

CHAPTER 4

*E*lizabeth's heart was in her throat as she watched Alec march toward Lindley. The forbidding snarl on Lindley's lips died in the face of Alec's angry expression. She felt at fault somehow. Should she step in? So much more was at stake than Alec realized. Lindley would provoke him, and if anyone saw the confrontation, that would reflect badly on Alec, proving to everyone that he was as Lindley claimed—nothing but a barbaric Scot.

"D-Don't," she called, not knowing exactly which man she spoke to and doubting if either would listen. Lindley gave her a black look before he faced Alec, fists clenched. Elizabeth stepped closer so she could hear what they were saying, but Alec waved her away.

"I've seen enough of your English backbone today," Alec said firmly, focusing on Lindley. "Go home. You've done enough."

Lindley shook his head, not giving an inch. "I've given you fair warning. You're not welcome in Lady Elizabeth's company any longer. I'm practically her fiancé and won't have her reputation besmirched by the likes of you. If a good pummeling is the only way to make you understand that, well, I'm ready to oblige."

Alec took off his hat and tossed it to the ground. Planting his feet, he looked ready for anything Lindley might do, but didn't raise his own fists. Instead, he regarded Lindley coolly. "I'd hate to soil your beautifully laundered cravat with your blood, but if you insist, I have no other recourse."

Elizabeth couldn't take her eyes off him. He was magnificent. Alec stood there, a gentle breeze playing with the hair that had come loose from his queue. And though he was calm, he definitely wasn't making idle threats.

Lindley assessed the situation and saw what Elizabeth did—that he was at the disadvantage. With a grunt, he changed course and tried to push past Alec toward Elizabeth. Alec caught his arm and pulled Lindley close so they were nearly nose to nose.

"*Practically* a fiancé is not the same as having signed all the settlements. If her father finds out you upset her today, it will not bode well for your suit." From the way Lindley was grimacing, Alec's grip must have been punishing. "Insult me all you want but have a care for her feelings."

Elizabeth's heart wrenched at Alec's words. Her father wouldn't set aside Lindley's suit for upsetting her. The duke had chosen a husband for her, and secretly, Elizabeth suspected he merely wanted her away from his household where he wouldn't have to hear her stutter any longer.

Lindley twisted his lips into an ugly grimace. "I know what a Scot like you wants. You probably heard the exorbitant amount her father is offering as her dowry, and you've decided to take it for yourself," Lindley growled, jerking his arm away.

Alec shook his head in disgust. "What are you blathering on about, man? I don't want or need her dowry. Besides, she is more valuable than any monetary assets."

Lindley stared at Alec for a moment before laughing in his face. "Valuable? She's valuable to me, all right. With every failed Season, her dowry was raised to tempt the gentlemen, but no one will offer for a woman who's practically a mute and can hardly attend society functions, much less be a hostess for one. But our fathers made a deal that suits me nicely." He sneered at Elizabeth. "All I require of the *lady* is to deliver her large dowry and an heir. For that to occur, no words are required. And once that's done, she can retire to one of my estates in the country and I'll come back to Town for my own entertainments."

Elizabeth was rooted to the spot at his crude and insulting comments. Anger rushed through her, making her breath come hard and fast. She stepped forward and pulled off her right glove, her body moving as if by its own accord. All she could think of was hurting him as much as he'd hurt her.

Lindley's sneer turned to a smirk. "Come to fall all over me with your thanks for being the only man alive willing to be leg-shackled to you?" he taunted.

She slapped his face as hard as she could, then turned away. Her palm stung more than she'd expected, but the pain was worth it.

Before she could step away, his hand snaked out and grabbed her arm. "You'll pay for that," he said, yanking her back against his chest.

"Unhand the lady," Alec demanded. He bolted forward, but Lindley dug his fingers deeper into her soft flesh until Elizabeth let out a yelp of pain.

"In a few short weeks, I'll own her," Lindley growled, his face close to hers. "I can do as I please."

He twisted her arm behind her back, and pain shot through her shoulder. Fear replaced her anger at his callous regard. Her throat closed, and she gasped for air. With her heart pounding wildly, it was impossible to form any words. All she could do was whimper like a child.

"Her father will hear of this," Alec said, his fists clenched. "Let her go."

Lindley laughed and shoved her forward. She fell into Alec's protective embrace and nearly cried with relief.

"It's won't matter what she tells the duke. He's made an agreement with my father that he'll not want to break. Our courtship and marriage will go on as planned." Lindley straightened his cuffs. "And since my father has the ear of the Prince Regent, *my lord*, you may want to think of the consequences before you cross me. It wouldn't be beyond my family's influence to make sure every good family in London gives the cut direct to the new Earl of Suffield and his mother. Do you understand?"

"You w-wouldn't dare." Elizabeth's heart sank even as she managed to get the words out, but she knew he would. Lindley's title and his father's standing among the *ton* would provide him an easy way to hurt Alec and Isabella. The cut direct was a death knell, and they would both be ostracized from all good society.

She felt Alec's arms tighten around her shoulders before he shifted to the side and stepped away from her. Of course he had to put distance between them, but she felt the loss of his warmth as keenly as she would feel the loss of his friendship. She hugged herself and rubbed her sore shoulder. Her entire life she had been hoping for love and kindness. She'd had a glimpse of that kindness for a brief moment with Alec but had to let it go. He'd become too important to her in the short time they'd been acquainted to allow him to sacrifice his standing, and his mother was too lovely to be caught in Lindley's hostility.

Once she was safely behind him, Alec confronted Lindley. "Are you threatening my mother?" His voice was deadly soft.

"Did I stutter? I have been in company with Lady Elizabeth

quite a lot lately." Lindley laughed at his own joke, but sobered quickly. "Let me be clear. Stay away from Lady Elizabeth, or you and your mother will pay the price."

"Aye, I understand," Alec said, right before he smashed his fist into Lindley's jaw. The man went down as if he'd been shot. Alec stood over him, righteous fury on his face. "And here's what you should know. No one threatens my family or they face me."

Lindley answered with a groan. "You'll regret this." He held his cheek and tried to sit up. "I'll make sure of it."

"I'm sure you will. I'll escort Lady Elizabeth home now, and, rest assured, we will be having an interview with her father the moment we arrive. Surely he won't want a blackguard such as yourself as a relation." Alec carefully stepped back and shook his head in disgust before he took Elizabeth's arm and left Lindley in the dirt.

Tess was coming down the path, but Alec didn't wait. He led Elizabeth to the walkway leading out of the park, and she was grateful that he was escorting her quickly toward the exit. She didn't want to see anyone of her acquaintance right now. She couldn't bear to perform the social niceties when her shoulder throbbed and she couldn't gather her thoughts. The man she'd been promised to freely admitted he only wanted her dowry and didn't plan to be faithful. They'd never make a love match and there could be no happiness in her life with a man like that. He'd called her a *mute*. Her cheeks burned with shame. She wanted to go to her father and beg for a reprieve, but it would likely do no good. And if she didn't end her acquaintance with Alec, both he and his mother would suffer. How could she watch them be ostracized because of her? And how could she marry a man as vile as Lindley?

"I'm sorry, lass. I truly am." Alec's voice was laced with concern.

Her throat clogged with tears and she couldn't speak, misery pooling in her middle. Alec's kind face and his worry for her were the last straws, and a sob escaped. He groaned when her first tear fell and took her arm to guide her to a more secluded spot.

"Tess, go and find the grooms," he instructed her maid, who trailed a few steps behind them. "Tell them we're ready to leave." Tess looked concerned at leaving Elizabeth when she was obviously distressed, so Alec hurried to assure her. "Don't worry. I'll be very careful with your mistress and her reputation."

Alec guided Elizabeth a little farther into a small copse of trees, where they had a bit of privacy from the popular paths but were still visible if someone looked for them. He pulled her to his chest. "Dinna cry, wee one."

But that was exactly what she did, wetting his shirtfront with her tears. How could Alec not look upon her with pity now? And how was she to marry Lindley, knowing how the cad truly felt about her?

After the tears slowed, Elizabeth cleared her throat and raised her head, hardly daring to meet his eyes. "I'm s-sorry."

"For what? Giving a magnificent set-down to a man who deserved it?" Alec gently slid his hands down her arms and ended at her elbows, keeping her in a loose embrace. "Do ye feel better?"

"No. I'm w-worried," she admitted, trying to ignore the jolt of awareness that went through her at his nearness and the intimacy of the moment. His height and bulk were like a shelter that she could find refuge in. "He could tell vicious l-lies about you and your m-mother. I'd hate to be the reason either of you were given the cut d-direct. That would be d-devastating for you both."

"Let me take care of that," he said with a shake of his head. "But I'm not concerned about me or my ma right now. I'm worried about you."

She held her hands to her cheeks and looked up at him to see if he was funning with her. How could he not be concerned about his social standing? A reputation could open or close doors for a family and everyone in it. Yet his eyes had nothing in them but care for her feelings. Her brow furrowed in confusion. No gentleman had paid her such attention, and she was unsure how to react.

"How's your hand?" he asked, taking her still ungloved fingers in his own and stroking her knuckles with his thumb.

His soothing circles sent tingles rippling up her arm and Elizabeth was glad she hadn't put her glove back on, yet. She looked down at his tanned hand holding hers, wishing he'd never let go. "I've n-never struck anyone before."

Alec chuckled. "It was a smashing debut, my lady. In the future, close your fist and aim for the nose."

Elizabeth shuddered slightly, still a bit horrified at her own actions. "Hopefully there will n-never be an occasion to use that b-bit of information."

He reached for her other hand, plucked out her glove and stuffed it into his coat pocket. When that was out of the way, he reached for her hands and brought them against his chest. "I'm proud of ye, lass."

Her heart thumped at his praise, but the thrill died quickly, and she dropped her gaze. "He didn't l-lie, Alec." She ducked her head. "N-No one offered for me in two Seasons, and I don't like going to social events. I . . . My t-tongue gets tangled, and I c-can't speak to gentlemen."

He squeezed her hands. "Och, you make your thoughts known just fine to me. I dinna speak like a proper Englishman, but you can still understand me. That's all that matters."

"I love your b-brogue," she said softly, hardly able to believe that her stutter didn't matter to him. Looking into his eyes, heat raced through her veins, radiating out from where his hands clasped hers. Awareness arced between them and she wanted to move closer to him. Much closer. "What a p-pair we are."

His gaze lingered on her mouth, and she closed her eyes, breathing in the scent of him—sunshine, horse, and mint. Her body swayed toward him ever so slightly, and he pulled her into his arms.

"Elizabeth," he said, his voice hoarse. "I want . . ."

She opened her eyes and lifted her face, her attraction to him mixing with hope that he wanted the same thing she did. "Y-Yes?"

His eyes were focused solely on her, making her feel as if she were the only woman in the world. She wanted his kiss—wanted *him*. Their connection was something she'd never felt with any other gentleman. She laid her palm on his chest, and his heart was pounding as hard as hers. "Alec?"

He groaned and let out a long breath. His fingers reached out to touch her cheek, as if he still needed even a small connection between them but wished for more. She did, too, and leaned her head into his palm, feeling forever changed. For the first time in her adult life she felt wanted, stutter and all.

Sounds of female laughter and the jingling of carriage horses from the park and the walkway behind them intruded, reminding her they were still in public and could be seen. Alec seemed to become aware of the fact at the same time. He cleared his throat and took a step back, albeit reluctantly.

"Elizabeth, we need to talk about Lindley." The name was like a cold bucket of water tossed over her head. She shivered and Alec took her hand again. "I'm worried about him havin' leave to court ye," he said, tracing a circle over the back of her fingers. "I know he said that your fathers have struck a deal, but can ye speak to your father about being released from it? After what happened today, that would be reasonable."

She could hardly think with Alec so near, but at the mention of her father, her ribcage squeezed. "He w-won't listen to me." Her voice was barely above a whisper. "He has no p-patience if I get stuck on a w-word."

"I could speak to him for ye," Alec offered. "Tell him what happened here today with Lindley." He glanced behind them, as if the bounder might be there and he'd have an opportunity to finish him off.

"I d-don't want your mother hurt by Lindley," Elizabeth said, leaning away, wishing she could change the subject. "And I know you d-don't, either, but I have enjoyed our friendship."

"I have as well and it won't bother us to lose a few friends in England. But, lass, I couldn't stand to see ye married to the likes of him. Ye must speak to your father or let me do so on your behalf." Alec's voice had a thread of pleading in it. "Please."

"I'll t-try to speak to him," she said, courage rising in her. "And I'd like to stay friends if you're not w-worried about Lindley's threat."

"Not worried in the least," he said, giving her a half-smile before he let go of her fingers. She nearly protested at the loss of his touch, wanting to hold onto him for a little longer, but she could hear horses coming their way. And though they were techni-cally in a public setting, they were still secluded and without a chaperone. Being caught alone with Alec would have repercus-sions for them both, so she let her hand drop to her side.

"I'd like to see ye happy, lass. Will ye still come and call on my mother and Kitty?" Alec's face was in earnest. "I promise ye, after an hour with them, ye'll feel happier than a sheep in a field of clover."

Elizabeth knew she should say no. The proper thing to do would be to go home and change her clothes, perhaps do some embroidery to please her mother, but he'd defended her today, comforted her, put her happiness before his own. She'd never felt so accepted, and she didn't want that feeling to end just yet. "I'd love to."

She slipped her glove back on, and when she was ready, Alec held out his arm. It didn't take long to walk to where Tess and the grooms were waiting with the horses.

"Are you well, my lady?" Tess asked, looking Elizabeth over.

"I'll be f-fine. I've decided to take t-tea at Suffield House," she said.

Tess bobbed her head. "Yes, my lady. Would you like to return home first and change out of your riding habit?"

Elizabeth considered her answer. If she returned home, her mother might demand her presence for tea or another gown fitting, and she'd never be allowed back out to Suffield House. "No, I won't be l-long, and I d-don't think Miss Kitty will m-mind if I call in my riding habit."

"She won't mind at all," Alec assured her as they moved to the horses.

Before a groom could assist Elizabeth onto her mount, Alec placed his hands at her waist and lifted her into the saddle. The heat of his palms was like a brand on her body, and her heart began to beat in double time, as if coming to life under his touch. Her gaze drifted to his lips. How would they feel on hers? She glanced down at Alec and he gave her a knowing smile, as if he knew the direction of her thoughts. She willed herself not to blush and quickly ducked her head to arrange the reins in her hands.

They rode side by side to Suffield House, and for just a moment, Elizabeth allowed herself to imagine that Alec—tall and handsome, full of smiles and a hypnotizing brogue that she could happily listen to for hours—was courting her. It was a beautiful dream of having the love of such a man, but a torturous one, knowing she was promised to Lindley.

She'd think on that later when alone in her room, trying to

come up with a plan to face her father and refuse Lindley's suit. Right now, in Alec's presence, she wanted to bask in the way he calmed and steadied her with his companionship and care, as well as how he stirred her senses as no one else ever had.

Before long they were in front of Suffield House, and Alec was at her side, ready to help her dismount. Her pulse pounded as he helped her down, and they shared a smile. Was he as affected as she was?

Watching him hand the horses off to a groom, Elizabeth picked up her skirts and waited for Alec's escort into the house. They were met at the door by a well-dressed butler.

"Banks," Alec nodded to the man. "Where might my mother be?"

"In the garden, my lord." He looked at Elizabeth and Tess. "Shall I have Cook bring some refreshment for the ladies?"

"Yes, and serve it in the garden," Alec instructed, cupping Elizabeth's elbow to lead her through the house.

"Would the lady's maid prefer to wait belowstairs?" Banks asked, giving Tess a kindly smile.

"If that is acceptable," Tess answered, looking to Elizabeth for permission.

"Of course," Elizabeth said, leaning closer to Alec. The excitement of the day was starting to catch up with her, and her knees felt like jelly. This morning had not turned out at all as she'd imagined. A spot of tea sounded like just the thing.

Alec led her to the back terrace and opened the door with one hand while keeping her close with the other. "Right through here."

The door opened into a garden, and Alec's hand slid from her elbow, his fingers closing around hers as they started down the gravel path. Even through her gloves, his warmth was like a heated glow from her hand straight to her heart. "My mother has a favorite bench just around the corner."

The winding path cut through shaded and sunny areas, with benches and statues set strategically throughout the flowers and trees. The garden was beautifully kept.

Elizabeth breathed deeply. "I l-love the s-smell of roses and lilacs."

Alec's mouth curved into a smile and he drew her deeper into the garden. "Did ye know the Celts consider the lilac magical because of its intoxicating fragrance?"

She grinned at his boyish exuberance. "Do you b-believe that kind of tale?"

"Aye." He winked and she couldn't restrain a laugh.

They turned a corner and his mother looked up from the bench where she sat reading. Her eyes lit when she saw Alec, but she quickly stood the moment she realized Elizabeth was with him.

"My lady," she exclaimed, putting her book down on a small stone table next to her. Kitty barked once before running to greet Elizabeth herself.

Elizabeth bent to receive some exuberant dog kisses. "Why, h-hello little l-lady." The dog gave her one last kiss before she would allow Elizabeth to pet her.

"It's a marvel," Isabella remarked. "My Kitty doesn't usually take to strangers."

Alec agreed, but his lips twitched as he held in his smile. "I've never been sure of her judge of character until now."

Elizabeth gave Kitty an extra scratch behind the ears. "She's a d-dear. Alec promised I'd feel b-better if I spent some time with her, and it's working already."

"Are you unwell?" Isabella asked, moving to Elizabeth's side, concern etched on her face. "Alec, has something happened?"

Elizabeth shook her head, embarrassed she'd mentioned being out of sorts. "N-No, it's not that. I m-merely had an unpleasant encounter with a gentleman in the p-park this morning, and your son was my champion."

Isabella looked at Alec proudly. "I'm glad to hear it, but I'm sorry you were distressed."

Alec was about to say something, but Mrs. Jennings appeared behind him, bearing a tray, a large smile on her face. "Your tea, my lady."

The housekeeper scooted Isabella's book over so she could set the tray on the table. Alec moved closer to look at the food.

"Shortbread," he said, his eyes lighting up as he sniffed the air. "And fresh! I haven't had a good shortbread since we left Scotland." He picked up a cookie off the tray and took a bite.

Mrs. Jennings looked pleased. "I hope you like it, my lord."

"It's perfect," he said, finishing the remaining portion. "You and Cook spoil me."

Elizabeth watched Alec interact with the servant and could hardly hold in her surprise. She'd never seen such companionability between family members and servants. It was wonderful to witness, and she wished she could carry the feeling to her own home.

"Can I t-try this Scottish d-delicacy?" she asked, setting Kitty on the ground.

Alec quickly brought her a plate with shortbread and cakes on it. "Tell me true, lass, if that shortbread isn't a little bit of heaven."

She laughed and raised her eyebrows, happiness bubbling through her. "You may not like my answer."

"I will, because I know you'll agree with me." Alec motioned toward the shortbread. "But if you need a little extra taste to it, we'll pretty it up for the best of both countries and dip my Scottish shortbread in your English tea."

She looked at the shortbread in her hand and gingerly took a bite. Chewing slowly, she watched as both Alec and his mother waited expectantly for her verdict. She swallowed and daintily brushed the crumbs from her fingers. "I think Scotland m-may win the day. This is so light and b-buttery, there's n-no need for tea."

Alec smiled triumphantly. "I knew you were a canny lass."

Isabella and Alec laughed along with her, and Elizabeth warmed. Their genuine friendship and her connection to Alec gave her confidence, something she'd rarely felt in her life. The strength of the feeling gave her much needed hope that she could find the courage for the biggest battle yet to come—facing her father about Lindley.

CHAPTER 5

Alec didn't particularly care for the theater, but his mother had been excited to see *Macbeth* performed, and he'd been anxious for a glimpse of Elizabeth, so he'd come. He hadn't seen her at any society functions for the last week and worried that something was wrong. Was she ill? Avoiding society? After Lindley's treatment of her, Alec hoped she'd been able to convince her father to rescind permission to court her.

The Duke and Duchess of Barrington entered their box, and a ripple went through the crowd. They were across the way from Alec's box, which gave him a good view. He didn't see Elizabeth right away, but when he did, he was stunned to see her enter on the arm of the Earl of Lindley. Why was she with him? What had gone wrong?

"Is everything all right?" his mother asked. Her eyes followed his. "Ah. Lady Elizabeth has arrived."

Alec folded his arms across his chest. "With that *eejit*, Lindley. He's the man who upset her in the park last week." And the man who had grabbed Elizabeth's arm and threatened Alec's mother. Lindley shouldn't be around either of the women he cared about.

"You never did explain what happened that day," his mother said, leaning closer, as if he were about to impart a great secret.

He barely heard her, unable to take his eyes off Elizabeth as she was escorted to her seat. Dressed in a toffee-colored gown with a lacy, cream-colored shawl draped around her shoulders, she looked finer than a good Scottish whisky on a cold night. He was spellbound as he watched her, and it was all he could do to remain in his seat and not go to her. The moment in the park where she'd been both fierce and vulnerable had pulled at something deep inside him---and turned his thoughts to what it would be like to kiss her. That idea had occupied him far too often each day and even in his dreams at night. She enchanted him like no other woman ever had. While they obviously both felt lacking in speech, none of that mattered when they were together. Her smile, her laugh, and the way she cared for others spoke volumes to him. Her smile was noticeably absent tonight, however.

"Alec?" his mother prompted.

"He didn't like Elizabeth being seen with me," Alec said, holding out a palm and wishing he could wave his hand and make Lindley disappear. "He has no love for Scots."

His mother's gaze turned anxious, and she laid her hand on his arm. "What precisely did he say?"

Alec didn't want to upset his mother but found it hard to hide his feelings on the matter. "He was rough with Lady Elizabeth and said that since he was practically her fiancé, he could decide if she associated with me or not."

Isabella wrung her hands, her gaze darting from Alec to the Barrington box. "Oh dear. How awful for Elizabeth."

Yes, it was, and after seeing her tears and hearing her assurance that day that she would talk to her father, he couldn't help but think something had happened in the week since they'd shared shortbread in his mother's garden. He had to talk to her, but the curtain went up.

The play turned his mother's attention, but Alec couldn't keep his eyes from Elizabeth. She looked uncomfortable seated directly in front of her parents. Lindley was at her side, subtly crowding her, sitting with his shoulder touching hers. Alec noticed how she leaned away from him. With a frown, Alec folded his arms, his fingers flexing. Could no one sense her discomfort?

The play seemed to go on interminably, and Alec couldn't concentrate. As soon as the curtain came down for intermission, he turned to his mother. "Shall I escort you to say hello to Elizabeth and her parents?"

She watched his face carefully, obviously seeing through his ruse, but agreed to his plan anyway. "Of course."

Mixing with the crowds, they made their way across the theater to the Barrington box. When they were admitted, Alec was relieved to find Elizabeth and her mother alone.

The ladies stood, and Alec bowed low. "Your Grace," he said to Elizabeth's mother. She nodded in acknowledgment and he turned to the woman he couldn't stop thinking about. "Lady Elizabeth," he said. "How are you enjoying the theater this evening?"

Elizabeth's eyes lit up and she curtsied. "Lord Suffield, Lady Suffield, how nice to see you again."

She rose, and Alec took note of the dark smudges that marred the skin beneath her eyes, testifying to missed hours of sleep. Her gown seemed to hang loosely on her frame as well, as if she'd lost weight. Alec's concern grew, but he couldn't say anything while in company.

As if she sensed his need to speak with Elizabeth alone, Isabella moved toward the duchess. "My lady, if I may, could I ask your advice? I have been admiring your gowns. Would you share the name of your *modiste?*"

"I'm happy to, Countess, but she's very exclusive, you know." The duchess opened her fan and arched a brow. "She serves only the finest ladies in society."

"I see. Well, I shall have to contact her directly. I must order an entire new wardrobe and wish only for the best workmanship for my gowns." She gave Alec a subtle nod as she led Elizabeth's mother to the corner.

When the two older women were safely out of hearing range, Alec moved closer to Elizabeth. "I've looked for you at the last few musicales and soirees, but never saw you at any of them. Are you well?"

"I'm w-well enough." She played with the edging on her sleeve before she met his gaze. "Entertainments are . . . still d-difficult for me."

"I see," Alec said, running a hand over his jaw. She was every inch a duke's daughter tonight, polite and remote. Anger at Lindley and worry for Elizabeth warred within him. "Well, I'm glad to see you here this evening, then."

What should he do? Politely withdraw? No. He needed to know she was all right, but they didn't have much time to converse before her father and Lindley returned.

Just as he was about to voice his concern, she lightly touched his forearm and favored him with a small smile. "If I were to t-take you into my c-confidence, however, my lord, I've been l-longing for a ride across the f-fields and a chance to shout at the sky."

Alec's thoughts went back to her wish for freedom. If he was allowed, he would do all in his power to grant that to her, although it was *his* wish to be the one at her side to share it. "Perhaps we could shout at the ceilings in my ballroom. The earl who commissioned the murals enjoyed wee bairns floating in a sky full of puffy, white clouds with arrows. They look quite forlorn. Shouting at the sad paintings could do us both good."

Elizabeth laughed as he'd hoped she would, but her smile didn't last as the box curtain opened to reveal the duke and Lindley returning with drinks in their hands. When Lindley's gaze landed on Alec, his eyes narrowed, and he marched toward them.

"I thought I made myself clear," he said as he nearly shoved a glass of lemonade into Elizabeth's hand. "You're not welcome to pay addresses to my fiancée."

The duke was speaking to his wife and didn't hear Lindley, but Elizabeth stiffened at Alec's side.

"The settlements are signed, then?" Alec asked with a raised brow.

Lindley looked uncomfortable for a brief moment before he waved his hand airily in Alec's face. "A mere formality."

"A formality that counts." Alec folded his arms, and Lindley flinched at the movement. Good. He obviously remembered their last meeting and the thumping he'd received.

The duke joined them, staring pointedly at Alec. Elizabeth stepped forward to make the introductions before Lindley could say anything. "F-Father, this is L-Lord Suffield."

Alec bowed, but the duke merely gave him a once-over. "I knew your grandfather," he said finally. "We had many long conversations at the club about how disappointed he was in his younger son's marriage."

Alec's mother had just taken his arm. He heard her intake of breath at the duke's words.

"I can't imagine why," Alec said, trying to hide his annoyance. "His younger son married the granddaughter of the Duke of Argyll."

"A *Scottish* duke," Elizabeth's father said. "There is a distinction."

"The Duke of Argyll is held in high regard and is a friend to the

Prince Regent," Alec countered. "Regardless, my parents were a love match." He looked at his mother and smiled. "And I had the best of parents."

His mother squeezed his arm and gave him a small smile. The duke snorted, shifting away from Alec and moving closer to Lindley. "Those are not always the most advantageous matches."

Alec looked at Elizabeth and saw the dismay on her face. It was very clear why Lindley was with her. The Duke of Barrington wasn't concerned with his daughter's well-being; he wanted an advantageous match and had decided that Lindley was it. Had he even given Elizabeth a chance to explain what had happened in Hyde Park?

"I respectfully disagree, Your Grace."

The duke quirked his brow and moved toward his chair, effectively dismissing them all.

Alec patted his mother's hand, still irritated at the duke's reaction, but the moment had passed, and the duke had moved on. Alec did the only thing he could—say goodbye to Elizabeth. "It was delightful to see you again, my lady."

She looked stricken. Her mouth opened and closed, but no words came out. Alec was powerless to do or say anything more. He watched Lindley grinning like a buffoon as he took Elizabeth's elbow to escort her back to her seat. Alec could only stare before ushering his mother into the passageway. He had to take a breath to keep himself from barging back into the box and putting himself between Lindley and Elizabeth. Walking away from her was more difficult than he'd imagined.

His mother didn't speak on the way back, but the tremble in her hands gave away her distress. He quickened his pace, wanting to help her to a seat.

"I'm sorry, Ma," he said as they reached their box and sat. The curtain had not yet risen, but his mother stared at the empty stage.

56

He reached for her elbow. "I didn't think the duke would speak like that."

Her lips curved slightly, as if she was trying to force a smile to her face, but it was too difficult. She gave up and pulled away to take a handkerchief out. "He's right, you know. I wasn't considered an advantageous match for your father."

He moved his chair closer to hers and put an arm around her. "I don't care what anyone thinks. You married the man you loved, and you were happy."

"Your father would have been so proud of you," she said, dabbing at her eyes with her hand-embroidered handkerchief that intertwined her initials with her husband's. "I wish he were here to smooth the way a bit."

Alec kissed her cheek. "If that were so, I wouldn't be here to need any smoothing. Not that I would mind giving the earldom to my da, mind you."

His mother patted his face. "You're doing a fine job. And the duke didn't say anything untoward, really. He just stated your grandfather's opinion."

Anyone maligning his mother made his temper flare, but he held himself in check for her sake. "Dinna let him make you feel anything less than the proud Campbell ye are," he said, a fierce edge to his voice. "We might have made England our home now, but there's still enough Scottish blood running through our veins to not let them trample our past or our future."

"You're right." She sat taller in her seat as the curtain rose again. "Thank ye," she whispered, allowing herself a moment to speak as she would have at home. The words made Alec's heart twist. She'd sacrificed everything for him so he could have lands of his own, and he wouldn't let anyone hurt her.

Looking across the way to the box where Lindley sat, still much too close to Elizabeth for Alec's liking, he clenched his fists. Had the man whispered in the duke's ear about Alec or his mother? Is that why he'd acted so boorish? Or was it merely as the duke said —a conversation he'd had with Alec's grandfather?

Alec would probably never know. Lindley would revel in Alec's discomfort, thinking it would drive his threat deeper into Alec's mind.

He watched Lindley reach his arm around Elizabeth on the pretext of adjusting her shawl. She flinched at his touch. Alec wanted to protect her from the obviously unwanted advances, but he couldn't, and Lindley well knew it. He was laughing at Alec's vexation over the duke's comments and flaunting his near-fiancé status.

When Lindley met Alec's eyes across the theater, he smiled and held up his drink in salute. The bounder thought he'd won, but Alec wasn't ready to concede the field just yet. His ancestors had led many a Highland charge with a war cry that struck fear in the hearts of their enemies.

And while Lindley thought he'd won the battle tonight, the war was far from over.

CHAPTER 6

*E*lizabeth pretended to browse the bookshelves at Hatchard's, but she couldn't focus on the titles. Last night's events at the theater had been so distressing, they were all she could think about. She closed her eyes, not wanting to remember the hurt on Isabella's face when her father had carelessly maligned her marriage. It was as if she'd betrayed Isabella's friendship by saying nothing. But the most upsetting part of the evening had to be when her father had simply dismissed Alec. She couldn't calm herself quickly enough to get any words out, and Alec had walked away. Her father's actions had stood in the face of her silence, and she could only imagine what Alec thought of her now.

Elizabeth leaned against the shelf, massaging the ache in her temple as it mingled with the ache in her heart. If she could call on Alec and Isabella to apologize, she would, but that wouldn't be proper. All she could do was relive the entire scene over and over and wish she'd reacted differently—that she'd told her father to stop or said a comforting word to Isabella. With a sigh, she wished her bosom friend Alice were here right now to help her decide the best course of action. Thankfully, she and her new husband would arrive in town tomorrow. Elizabeth could hardly wait to see her.

Deciding to go home and drown in despair from the comfort of her own sitting room, Elizabeth moved around the corner and nearly bowled over another patron. Steadying both of them by grabbing a bookshelf, she was surprised to find herself looking at Alec's mother.

"I'm s-so sorry," she said, gripping the shelf even harder, as dread poured over her. What if Isabella was angry with her?

"Lady Elizabeth, I do hope you're all right," Isabella said, as she clutched Elizabeth's arm. "My apologies. I wasn't looking where I was going."

"It's quite all right. Neither was I," she replied. This had to be Providence intervening, so she hurried to do the one thing she'd been thinking about since last night. "I w-want you to know how sorry I am for the w-way my father b-behaved last evening. I would not have your feelings hurt for the w-world."

Isabella smiled and patted Elizabeth's hand before stepping back. "You have such a good heart, my lady. I admit, his words stung, but Alec reminded me that I have nothing to be ashamed of. I loved my husband, and he loved me."

Something I'll never be able to say, Elizabeth thought. "My p-parents have an arranged marriage that is amicable at b-best. I don't think he believes in love m-matches."

"A pity," Isabella said, her eyes full of concern. "Alec mentioned you were being courted by Lord Lindley and that your father means to betroth you to him. Yours is not a love match, I presume?"

Elizabeth wished she could have heard that conversation between Isabella and Alec. Had he told his mother the details of what Lindley had said to her in Hyde Park? Did she know how humiliated Elizabeth had felt when he'd laughed and said he was the only man alive who would take a mute to wife?

"Yes, my f-father has given p-permission for the earl to court me." Which Lindley took great pleasure in reminding her of when no one was looking—including the fact that he wouldn't have any use for her once she'd given him her dowry and provided an heir.

She'd tried to speak to her father about the issue. Gathering her courage had taken an entire day, but she'd finally been able to ask for an interview. Before going, she'd rehearsed over and over how to tell him she refused to marry Lindley. But standing in front of his desk while he stared at her, nerves had overcome her best efforts, and she'd gotten exactly two sentences out before he'd tired of her stuttering.

"I can't understand you," he'd said. "And I don't have time for this just now." After that, he'd politely shown her to the door. It was apparent he hadn't even tried to listen to what she'd said.

Isabella lightly touched her forearm, bringing Elizabeth back to the present. "I heard there was a confrontation between Alec and Lord Lindley while you were riding in the park," Isabella continued, a bit tentatively.

Elizabeth bit her lip and looked around to make sure no one was nearby to overhear. She was almost too embarrassed to say the words aloud. "Lord Lindley c-carries a grudge against Highlanders. He's sure that Alec m-merely wants to steal me away like some savage."

"If I may be frank, my dear, I wouldn't object to that." She winked. "When we arrived in London, my son assured me he wouldn't have time for the social whirl, yet I've been escorted to a ball, soirees, musicales, and the theater. Of course, I don't believe he has suddenly developed a taste for England's entertainments. He enjoys your friendship and wants to be wherever you are likely to be."

Elizabeth stood rooted to the spot. Was Isabella admitting that Alec had a *tendresse* for her? Or was it simply friendship he wanted? Her heart hoped for the former, but she hardly dared to even think that. "I enjoy his c-company."

More than enjoyed it. He was the only man who'd ever looked past her stutter, and he was more than agreeable in conversation and appearance. She brought her hand to her lips and a flush crept up her neck, remembering how she'd imagined what it would feel like to kiss him. His strong arms surrounding her had been like a shelter in the storm. She'd felt safe, and for a handful of heartbeats, she'd gotten lost in his eyes, hope rising quickly in her chest that he truly would kiss her. Of course, he'd been too gentlemanly to do such a thing, but his soft touch of comfort had been a boon to her soul.

Isabella pulled her back to the present by linking her arm through Elizabeth's. "If it's not too much trouble, I'd like to invite you to tea. Alec is gone on estate business today, and Kitty would love to see you."

"That sounds d-delightful. If you're s-sure." Elizabeth moved toward the door, calmness flowing over her with Alec's mother by her side. It was nice to be with someone who didn't judge her and seemed to genuinely want to be her friend, no matter what her father had said or done.

"I'm sure." She squeezed Elizabeth's arm. "It would be a lovely diversion."

They quickly collected Tess, where she'd been waiting near the front of the store, and spoke to Elizabeth's carriage driver to send him home, before they all got into Isabella's coach.

"Tell me, how did you enjoy the play?" Isabella asked, as she arranged her skirts on the seat.

Elizabeth had hardly been able to concentrate on the play with Lindley doing all he could to appear the besotted suitor in front of her parents, while silently mocking her for knowing the truth with his barely concealed disdain when they weren't looking. "I thought the actors were p-particularly accomplished d-during the death scenes."

"My, yes," Isabella exclaimed. "Although the actor playing Macbeth seemed a bit shrill at times. 'Tomorrow aaand tomorrow aaand tomorrow,'" she quoted, raising her voice and drawing out the syllables.

Elizabeth smiled at her imitation. "It was g-good of you and the earl to g-greet us at intermission."

"Your mother was quite helpful in recommending her *modiste* to me. I plan to visit her later this week." Isabella looked down at her gown, still serviceable, but a bit out of date. "Fashions are slightly different here, and Alec has given me funds to have new gowns made."

"Madame V-Villiers has exquisite t-taste. I'm sure you'll be pleased." Elizabeth had spent many hours in the *modiste's* shop and had come to trust the woman's recommendations.

The carriage stopped in front of Suffield House, and the footman helped the ladies down. After they had removed their hats and gloves, and Tess was sent down to the kitchen for her own spot of tea, Isabella and Elizabeth settled in the drawing room decorated in blue and gold.

"This is one of my favorite parlors in the house," Isabella told Elizabeth as they sat on the settee near the hearth. A small fire burned, giving off just enough warmth to be comfortable. "It reminds me a bit of my sitting room at home."

"Do you miss Scotland t-terribly?" Elizabeth asked. She couldn't imagine leaving her home to settle so far away.

"Sometimes," Isabella admitted. "But Alec is here, so I'll stay to support him. We can visit Scotland, I'm sure. And we have fine neighbors," she added with a smile, tilting her head in Elizabeth's direction.

"I'm glad you still think so after my f-father's remarks last evening." Elizabeth leaned closer. "I hope you'll f-forgive me and my f-family."

Isabella patted her arm. "Already forgotten, my dear." They both looked up as Mrs. Jennings brought in a tray, then quietly quit the room. "And we'll have tea and cakes as good friends do, for I hope you consider me a friend."

Elizabeth nodded, happiness bubbling through her. "Yes, of c-course." She watched as Isabella poured, grateful for her easy acceptance.

"How do you take your tea?" she asked, her hand hovering over the sugar bowl.

"A dash of m-milk and one sugar," Elizabeth told her, settling back in her seat. Each time she'd visited Suffield House, she'd found herself able to relax and enjoy herself. It wasn't an easy feat for someone who normally preferred being alone with her sketch-book and almost always hoped to avoid notice.

Isabella handed Elizabeth her tea and made a cup for herself. "Tell me more about your family. Have you any brothers or sisters?"

"No, I am my parents' only living child. My m-mother had two boys that both died soon after their birthing. The physician t-told my mother she was lucky not to have perished as well." Elizabeth took a sip of her tea, surprised her stutter seemed so easily controlled for the moment. The more comfortable she grew, the more the stutter eased. "Is Alec your only child?"

"Yes. His father came down with consumption when Alec was small and passed away shortly after." Sadness shadowed Isabella's eyes. "I wish they could have had more time together—that our family could have had more time together."

She sounded so wistful that Elizabeth's heart twisted with sympathy. "I'm sorry to have m-mentioned it."

"No, it's quite all right." Isabella set her tea down and put a smile on her face. "Tell me more about your interests. Do you play the pianoforte? Or draw, perhaps?"

"Well, I do enjoy d-drawing portraits," Elizabeth said. "Of people and animals."

Isabella's eyes widened and she clapped her hands. "Would you ever consider drawing Kitty for me? I would love to have a portrait of my precious girl."

"Och, what is this madness, Ma? Commissioning a portrait of the dog before one of me, your dear son?" Alec said with a chuckle as he entered the sitting room.

He bussed his mother's cheek and walked over to stand in front of Elizabeth. He looked windblown, as if he'd lost his hat during a horse race and hadn't bothered to retrieve it. Everything about him drew Elizabeth in—his presence, his smile, and the way he was looking at her.

He bowed and took her hand, lifting it to his lips. "Good morning, my lady."

"Good morning," she murmured, watching his lips touch her skin, tingles skittering up her arm and pooling in her chest. She had hardly stopped thinking of his tender touches in the park and her pulse thrummed at their renewed contact.

"Am I to understand that my mother has asked you to draw a portrait of Kitty?" he asked, as he took a seat in the armchair across from Elizabeth. He crossed one ankle over the other, legs outstretched, as he settled in and got comfortable. He was definitely a man at ease with himself.

"Y-Yes," she said, her blush deepening. "If that is agreeable to you."

Alec looked at his mother, then back at Elizabeth. "It is, on one condition: that I be allowed at the sitting. I can't wait to see how you'll keep Kitty in one position for longer than a minute."

"You're welcome to observe how I work," Elizabeth said, lifting the corners of her mouth in amusement. "But I assure you, you will find it tedious."

"My Kitty is very accomplished," Isabella said with a glance at Alec. "She can be high-spirited, but knows when to sit still."

Alec chuckled and shook his head. "You mustn't tell falsehoods in front of our guest. That isn't proper."

Isabella pointed her finger, mock-scolding him. "Oh, you."

They laughed together as Kitty nosed her way into the room. She bypassed Alec and Isabella and went directly to Elizabeth, who reached down to pat the dog's head. "There's a good girl. You'll sit still for me, won't you?"

Kitty jumped up on the settee beside her, and Elizabeth petted the dog, while giving her an evaluation with an artist's eye. Kitty had a unique look with her long hair and soulful eyes that would make drawing her a pleasant challenge. Elizabeth was excited to get out her sketchbook and start.

Lost in thoughts of poses and possible bribes for Kitty, the chiming of the clock on the mantel brought her back to the present. Checking the time once more, she sighed. Her mother had admonished her not to dally at the bookshop and be home by eleven for callers. If she didn't leave now, she'd be late. With one final pat for Kitty, she stood, and Alec stood with her.

"Is something amiss?" His green eyes were looking into hers in such a way that she wanted to move closer, run her fingers through his black hair, and pull him down for a kiss.

Her heart raced at that wanton thought, and her words came out breathless, her stammer pronounced. "I h-h-have an appointment and m-must return home."

Alec didn't seem to notice her stumbling speech. He merely held out his arm. "Let me escort you."

Always the gentleman. She loved that about him.

Elizabeth slid her hand into the crook of his elbow. "Th-Thank you." Looking back at Isabella, she said, "And thank you for a d-delightful diversion today. If I m-may repay the f-favor tomorrow afternoon, I'd love your c-company when I t-tour the new Veterans Club with my f-friend Alice and her husband. It's a worthy, charitable v-venture."

Isabella moved Kitty off her lap and stood. "Oh yes, I'd like that. Alec served in the 74th Highlanders regiment. I'd be happy to help in any endeavor that helps veterans."

"As would I," Alec put in. "May I escort you ladies to the club?"

"Of c-course." Elizabeth looked up at him, wishing she'd seen him in his uniform. There was no doubt he would have been dashing. She'd heard stories of the Highlander bravery at Quatre Bras and Waterloo. Had Alec been there? "Your c-company would be appreciated, I'm s-sure. I shall c-call for you in my c-carriage just after luncheon."

"We'll be waiting." Isabella bestowed a smile mixed with motherly pride on Alec before she turned to Elizabeth. "Then, if there's time afterward, we can also make plans for Kitty's portrait."

"Yes, I'd l-like to get started on the c-commission." Elizabeth looked at Kitty who was curled up on one end of the settee, her head on the embroidered pillow in the corner, as if she was quite done in after her exertions of the day.

"Then it's settled." Isabella walked them to the drawing room doorway and gave Elizabeth one more wave goodbye. "Until tomorrow."

Alec led her into the foyer where Banks was waiting. "Lady Elizabeth must return home for an appointment. Would you fetch

Tess?" But before the butler could leave to do his bidding, Alec leaned in to stop his progress and added, "Slowly?"

The butler could hardly repress a grin. "Yes, my lord."

The moment Banks was out of sight, Alec drew Elizabeth into a small alcove near the door. Her insides fluttered when he touched her arm and stared down at her, as if memorizing every detail of her face. "I've been worried for ye."

Elizabeth couldn't form a single thought as her pulse started to pound in her ears. She stepped closer, unable to help herself wanting to be near his warmth and steadiness. "I'm so sorry about l-last night. My f-father . . ." She paused. "Your m-mother . . ."

He held a finger against her lips. "She knows you're not responsible for your father's actions, and she enjoys your company." His finger traced her cheek, slowly, deliberately, sending shivers down her spine. "*I* enjoy your company."

She looked up at him, feeling as if her heart would burst. "And I yours."

He bent down until his lips brushed her ear. "I can't stop thinking about ye. Yer laugh, yer courage, and the way ye love my mother's devilish dog. Ye undo me." His fingers stroked the back of her neck, and Elizabeth's knees turned to pudding. "I know it's a bit sudden, lass, but I'd like to ask your father for permission to court ye, Lady Elizabeth. I . . . I've never met anyone like you and I want the chance to bring you flowers and spout terrible poetry and make you laugh."

His eyes were uncertain, and Elizabeth reached her hands around his neck, drawing him scandalously close. "Oh, Alec," she breathed out. The idea that this handsome, funny, and honorable man wanted to court her made Elizabeth want to shout for joy, but she knew her father would never allow it. His mind was set on Lindley. "I w-would be honored, my lord, but my father might make things difficult."

"'Tis I who am honored." He kissed her temple and she inhaled his scent of mint with a touch of heather, as if he had a bit of the Scottish moors on his person. Comforting and exciting all at once. "And your father would have no reason to reject my suit," he added.

Elizabeth hoped that to be true. Surely her father would see the benefit of having two suitors for her hand and perhaps he would allow her to choose her husband. If he did, she would have no trouble with the decision. She couldn't get enough of the man in front of her.

Isabella's voice sounded down the hall behind her, greeting Tess. The spell was broken. Elizabeth reluctantly reminded herself that they were in front hall of Suffield House where any servant could observe them. She drew back, not missing the unhurried way Alec let her go. When only their hands were left touching, she squeezed his fingers and moved toward the voices.

They all met in the foyer, and Isabella acted as if Alec and Elizabeth had just left the sitting room and she'd followed them. She chattered on about plans for the portrait of Kitty, and when would be a good time to move forward, but Elizabeth hardly heard. Alec was going to ask her father for permission to court her! All her dreams finally seemed within reach, and Alec was at the center of them.

With another wave goodbye, Alec escorted Elizabeth down the street, Tess following behind them. She would be a few minutes late, but knowing Alec's feelings toward her was worth any cross looks from her mother.

Elizabeth glanced at her townhouse, but no carriages were out front. She supposed they could have been taken around to the mews. No matter, though, if she weren't there to greet the first callers with her mother. The only company she wanted was right beside her.

She tightened her grip on Alec's elbow, and he used his other hand to cover hers. When he looked down at her, the warmth in his eyes was unmistakable. "I'm looking forward to escorting you to the Veterans Club tomorrow. Are ye by chance attending the Berwick ball tomorrow night?"

"Yes, I am." She hadn't wanted to go where she'd be forced to play out the ridiculous courtship with Lindley, but the thought of a true courtship with Alec filled her with anticipation. "I'll m-make sure to save you a dance." Or two.

He lightly stroked her fingers. "I'd like that. A waltz, perhaps." His smile was just a tad bit wicked. What she wouldn't give to be able to read his thoughts.

She curled her toes inside her slippers. Fortune had finally smiled on her. "Of c-course."

Her happiness was short-lived, however, when she saw the Earl of Lindley's carriage at the far end of the street. Suddenly her mother's insistence that she be home at a certain time became clear. She'd known Lindley would be calling on her.

Alec saw the carriage at the same time she did. He scowled. "I don't like him near ye, and I can't fathom why your father allows it."

They didn't have much time if she wanted to be inside before Lindley arrived. "It w-won't be for much longer, hopefully. And I won't be left unchaperoned," Elizabeth assured him. "With my m-mother in attendance, he wouldn't dare approach me with even a hint of impropriety."

Alec let out a sigh. "Verra well. But I'm going to ask your father for an interview at his earliest convenience."

She chuckled as she looked up at the man beside her. He was everything she'd hoped for in a husband---someone she could dream of sharing a life and home with. "I c-can't think of anything I want m-more."

He held onto her arm for a half-second more, leaning close and breathing her in.

"You'll be late, my lady," Tess said, coming up on Elizabeth's other side.

Alec stepped back and bowed politely. "Of course. Until tomorrow," he murmured, for Elizabeth's ears alone.

"Yes, my l-lord." Anticipation rushed through her, and she couldn't keep back a smile. The day had started out gloomy, but was ending with the happiest moment of her life thus far. She closed her eyes to revel in the sensation and opened them to remind herself it wasn't a dream. "I'm l-looking forward to it."

He watched her until she was safely to the door, which made her heart melt a little. But the same heart hardened and shrank at the sight of Lindley's carriage as it stopped in front of her home. She quickly went inside and took off her bonnet and gloves, handing them to Tess. Steeling herself for her mother's ire and Lindley's visit, she walked up the stairs to the drawing room they always used to receive callers.

At her entrance, her mother glanced up from her needlepoint and frowned. "You are late, Elizabeth."

"Only j-just," she protested. Her heart was still racing, and she took a calming breath.

"Did you have a pleasant outing? Find any new books at Hatchard's?"

"No, n-nothing caught my eye t-today, Mama." Except for a handsome Highlander. Not that she could confide such a thing to her mother. Instead, Elizabeth sat down and arranged her skirts, just as their butler, Dawson, announced the Earl of Lindley.

"Send him in," Elizabeth's mother said.

Lindley appeared in the doorway, wearing a starched white shirt and cravat, but the rest of his ensemble was all black.

Matching the color of his soul, Elizabeth thought sourly.

He smoothed his already wrinkle-free waistcoat and bowed to the ladies. "Good morning," he said with a false smile directed at her mother, before he made his way to Elizabeth's side.

Drat. She should have sat in the chair instead of the settee. He crowded her once again, sitting much too close.

No one said anything for a moment, yet the air felt charged. Something was afoot, but Elizabeth didn't know what—until her mother put away her needlepoint and stood. "I must check with Cook about the menu for this evening. I'll return shortly."

Elizabeth felt a frisson of panic skitter over her, and she started to rise out of her seat as well. Lindley grabbed her arm and put enough pressure on it that she was forced to sit back down. "M-Mother," Elizabeth managed to get out, her alarm making speech impossible. "D-Don't . . ."

Her mother clucked her tongue. "I'll be right back, and the door will be open. Don't be a pea-goose. A couple needs a moment or two of privacy when they're courting." She winked at Lindley, and Elizabeth's heart sank. This had been planned, and there was nothing she could do.

As soon as her mother's heels receded down the hall, Elizabeth jumped up, but Lindley moved with her and held her arm in an iron-clad grip so she couldn't move away. "Now do you see how easy it would be to claim you have been compromised and that we must be wed at once? Then we could have a small ceremony and be done with it. I think both of your parents would support me, actually."

Elizabeth shook her head, bile rising in her throat. "I'll d-deny it."

"Who would believe you? Our fathers are quite anxious to see it done. It seems as if your family can't wait to be rid of you." He grabbed her chin roughly and lifted it. "You will be my wife, Elizabeth, our families allies, and your dowry will fill my coffers for years to come. I'll make sure of it."

Tears formed in Elizabeth's eyes. She jerked away, nearly stumbling. "You're a m-monster," she said, wishing she dared slap his face again.

"All you have to do is make this courtship look like all that is proper to the tabbies of the *ton*." he said, straightening his cuff. "Even *you* should be able to do that."

Clenching her fists, she backed up until she was near the door. The look on his face was that of a cat who had caught a bird and was playing with it before the kill. How could she fight a man with no scruples, a man determined to make her life one of misery and pain?

He took a step toward her, but she let out a little cry of dismay and turned, running from the room, his laughter echoing after her.

CHAPTER 7

*A*lec watched his mother with amusement. She'd been staring out the drawing room window waiting for a glimpse of Elizabeth's carriage for the last quarter hour. "Are you worried she won't come for us, Ma?"

"Of course not. Just excited for our outing, is all." She let the curtain drop and turned to face him. "I notice you are nicely turned out."

He inclined his head. "Thank you. My new valet is a wonder with a cravat." Alec had liked the man, but he did seem too serious by half. He had a mind to take it upon himself as a challenge to make the valet laugh.

"Oh, she's here!" His mother jumped up from her seat and quickly put on her gloves.

Alec stood and offered her his arm. "Shall we?"

They walked to the front hall and Alec's own excitement at spending the afternoon with Elizabeth unfurled the moment Banks opened the door and she stood in front of him dressed in a sunshine-yellow gown just a shade lighter than her hair. Her pelisse was a shade of lavender that made the yellow even more vibrant.

"Good afternoon," she said with a small curtsy and a smile.

"Good afternoon," Alec said, trying not to appear too eager. He offered her his other arm. "You look lovely. A bright spot in a dreary English day."

Elizabeth tilted her head up to glance at the sky, then back at him. "Th-thank you. I-I do hope it doesn't rain."

A liveried footman held the carriage door open for them. Alec helped Elizabeth in first, then his mother, before climbing in himself. When they were all comfortable, Alec rapped on the roof and the carriage started forward.

"Was Miss Kitty very put out to be left alone today?" Elizabeth asked his mother.

"Yes, but Mrs. Jennings was consoling her in the kitchen when we left." Isabella touched the curtain, as if she wanted one last glimpse of the townhouse before it was out of sight. "She is in very good hands."

Alec leaned forward. "Mrs. Jennings will sneak her morsels of shortbread. Kitty isn't afraid to show her good Scottish taste."

Elizabeth chuckled. "I think you've changed my taste as well. I've b-been craving shortbread since our d-day in the garden."

"You are welcome to come and get more anytime." Alec noted Elizabeth's countenance seemed as bright as her gown. He hadn't seen her this happy and lighthearted before. "Tell me about your friend we're going to meet today."

Elizabeth folded her hands in her lap as if she were about to embark on telling a long story. "Alice h-had her come-out the s-same year I did. She's the Duke of Huntingdon's daughter and one of the k-kindest people I know. No m-matter how many s-suitors she had swarming her at b-balls, she would always s-seek me out and introduce m-me to all of her acquaintants. And she was m-most sincere in her friendship. She never m-minded my speech hesitations at all."

Isabella reached out and patted Elizabeth's knee. "She sounds like a dear friend. The very best kind to have."

Elizabeth agreed and looked at Alec. "She recently married the Marquess of Wolverton and has been away on her wedding trip. I haven't seen her in several weeks and have been looking forward to our appointment this afternoon."

"I'm looking forward to making her acquaintance," Alec said, her obvious happiness spreading to him. Alice was obviously very dear to her, and he hoped to make a good impression.

"Oh, this must be the club," Elizabeth exclaimed as she looked out the window as the carriage slowed and came to a stop.

They were in front of a non-descript building on the edges of a middling neighborhood. Definitely not a Mayfair address, but more one for those of genteel poverty. Alec got out first and helped the ladies down. Tess and Elizabeth led the way and Alec escorted his mother.

They knocked on the door and a large man with a wicked scar running down the side of his face answered. "May I help you?"

The words were barely out of his mouth when a woman appeared behind him. "Reams, I'd like you to meet my most bosom friend, Lady Elizabeth."

"Alice." Elizabeth's smile was wide as the two women embraced. "I've missed you so."

"It seems an age since I've been in your company. I'm so glad you're a faithful letter writer." Alice hugged Elizabeth again. "Oh, I have so much to tell you." She looked behind her. "But first, will you introduce me to your friends?"

Elizabeth stepped aside. "Of course. Lady Wolverton, may I present the Earl of Suffield and Lady Suffield?"

Alec bowed and his mother curtsied. "Pleased to meet you, my lady," Alec said.

Alice inclined her head. "I've heard so much about you both. Thank you for coming."

A tall, well-dressed man met them in the entryway, and Alice held out her hand. "Ah, here is my husband, Lord Wolverton. This is the Earl of Suffield and his mother, Lady Suffield." She drew Elizabeth closer. "And this is Lady Elizabeth."

Lord Wolverton bowed over Elizabeth's hand. "I've heard so much about you, my lady, it's as if I know you already."

Elizabeth smiled and glanced at Alice. "And I, you, m-my lord. Your w-wife's letters are quite complimentary on your behalf."

Lord Wolverton's gaze landed on Alice as well. "For which I am most grateful." He turned slightly to greet Alec. "I've been looking forward to meeting more of Alice's friends. Please, won't you call me Christian? We're not much for titles while here in the club."

"Then I'm sure I'll enjoy being here. Please call me Alec." He pulled on his cravat. "London is much different from Edinburgh."

"I thought I detected a Scottish brogue." Christian turned to lead the way into the club. "How long have you been in England?"

"Just a few weeks. I recently came into my title." The ladies had begun conversing about Alice's wedding day, so Alec kept his attention on Christian. "Lady Elizabeth tells me your club is also a new addition to London."

"Yes." They walked down a hall with several doors leading off that looked like small parlors. Christian looked in each one as they passed. "When I came home from the war, I saw too many men who struggled to make a life back home when part of their souls had been left on the battlefield. This club is a place where they can find a brotherhood that will hopefully help them find a new beginning."

"Aye, those who served in the Scottish regiments experienced the same displacement. Only their troubles went a bit further when they came home from war to find their places burned out and their families gone." Alec tried to hide the bitterness creeping into his tone.

Christian put a hand on Alec's shoulder. "I've heard of the clearances. I'm sorry. We've all been fighting Old Boney for so long, and now we've come home to an entirely different world than the one we left. Tell me, where did you serve?"

Pride and some nostalgia for his clansmen filled him. "I marched halfway across Portugal and then into France with the 74th Highlanders. Where was your assignment?"

"I was in France for a time, but mostly in Spain." He led them into a large room and turned to wait for the ladies. "If I might interrupt for a moment, I wanted to give you a little tour of our establishment." He looked fondly at Alice. "As you might have seen as we walked down the hallway, there are reading rooms available with places set for conversation. But this is one of the club's more popular rooms."

They looked around at the pugilistic leather bags hanging from the ceiling in one corner. A man was punching one and looked very much absorbed in the activity, as if he didn't even realize there were other people in the room. The other corners featured billiards tables. A perfect combination for a gentleman's club.

"Do you have pugilism exhibitions?" Alec asked. He'd seen a few while in France and he'd heard of Gentleman Jackson's in London.

"No, the men mostly use the pugilism equipment to focus their energies." Christian was already moving back into the hall. "It's good for them to keep active."

"Do you have many patrons?" Isabella asked.

"Since we're only starting out, we've had to limit the member-ship for now. If you were to come back in the evening hours, you would find a crowd to rival White's. The Veterans Club has a waiting list already." Alice looked at her husband proudly. "We're already discussing ways we can accommodate more people."

"I'd like to help in any way I can," Alec said, very impressed at what Christian had been able to do for the veterans already. "It's a wonderful cause."

Christian led them into a large dining room. "We offer a free meal every day and have the best beefsteak and ale in the city." He turned to face the group. "If you'll wait here, I'll tell the cook we're ready for luncheon."

Alec helped the ladies into their seats and sat himself. He looked around the room at the other tables with men quietly talking. Christian's vision for a respite for veterans was inspiring, and Alec wanted to be part of it.

Two ladies accompanied Christian on his way back, laden with dishes. They set plates on the table that had a delicious smell wafting from them. Once Christian was seated, they ate the simple, but savory, fare.

Alec sat back in his seat. "I was skeptical of your claim to the finest beefsteak and ale, but I must say, you've the right of it. That was likely the best meal I've had since leaving Scotland."

"I'll not tell our cook of your treasonous words," his mother said, raising her eyebrows. "She might decide to leave us and then where would you be without your shortbread the way you like it?"

Alec held up his hands in mock surrender. "I wouldn't want to bring down her wrath upon my head, so I'll have to count on your vow of silence on the matter."

They all laughed.

Men were starting to fill the rest of the tables in the room. Alice touched Elizabeth's arm. "I have been serving lunch to the veterans with my new friend Lady Charlotte. Would you like to join us?"

"I would love to." Elizabeth turned worried eyes to Isabella.

"But I won't stay if you have another appointment. Would you mind being here a little longer?"

Isabella turned to Alec and tipped her head. "I would be honored to be included. Will the gentlemen be joining us?"

"I, too, would be honored to serve the veterans." Alec didn't want to leave this room or the cozy group of people surrounding him. Elizabeth was happy here and it showed in the glow of her face. The troubles with her father and Lindley seemed far away.

They all rose and went to the kitchen. The cook quickly found aprons for them and gave them instructions. Lady Charlotte soon joined them, and though they'd only just met, it was as if they'd all been friends for ages. Alec was content to watch and listen to the women as they chatted with the veterans who came through the luncheon line, though he soon had several new acquaintances of his own. As soon as the veterans found out he'd served in the Scottish regiments, men were happy to share their fond remembrances of the Scots and how proud they'd looked marching in their kilted ranks. A camaraderie soon sprang up between him and the English soldiers, though he'd never seen them before. A shared experience like war was a formidable bond.

A wizened, older man shuffled through the line, his unkempt beard nearly hiding his small eyes, which hardly left Elizabeth. Alec watched him carefully, just to make sure he meant no harm. When he came close to Alec, he motioned toward the lady, and his voice rasped out, "Do you know her?"

"I do," Alec confirmed. "That's Lady Elizabeth Barrington."

The other man pursed his lips and shook his head. "Knew her father, I did. Coward of the first order. Such a shock that something so beautiful could come from a man with no soul." The man shook his head and moved away, still muttering.

Alec wasn't sure what to make of his statement. He wanted to question the man further, but Elizabeth touched his arm. "I'm sorry, but I m-must return home to prepare for the Berwick b-ball this evening."

"I'm happy to escort you home." He scanned the room for the old man once again, but he'd disappeared in the crowd. The man's accusation of the duke being a coward was echoing in Alec's mind. He wanted to ask a few questions, but apparently he'd lost his chance. Instead, he focused on Elizabeth at his side. "Don't forget you've promised me a dance this eve, lass."

"I won't f-forget." Her eyes sparkled with happiness. "Thank you for c-coming today."

"It was my pleasure." He put his hand over hers. "I was glad to meet your friends."

"It has been a perfectly w-wonderful afternoon." She sighed and pressed closer to him. "I w-wish every day could be l-like this."

"I believe if your father accepts my suit, I can arrange that." He winked, and she laughed. Having her next to him felt right, as if they were parts of a puzzle that fit perfectly together. The longer he knew her, the easier it was to imagine her as his wife.

Her head leaned against his arm and he barely resisted pressing a kiss to her crown. "You are so k-kind," she said softly.

"It's easy to be kind when I'm in your company." They arrived at the front door where Reams was waiting with their coats and gloves. Alec helped Elizabeth on with hers, lingering a little longer as his fingers brushed her throat when he fastened the frogs. Her pulse fluttered underneath his knuckles and his own heart beat in time with hers.

Christian cleared his throat behind them. "I didn't know there was a race to the entrance," he said, arching his brows. "If I had, you wouldn't have gotten such a lead, but then, perhaps you wanted a moment alone."

Alec noticed Elizabeth blush at his words and he inclined his head in Christian's direction. "Don't mind him, my lady. The

English are often found lacking in conversation and manners. I won't hold it against him."

Christian laughed out loud. "Just like a Scot to be so bold, but it doesn't seem as if Lady Elizabeth objects, so we shan't mention it again."

Elizabeth flushed clear to the tips of her ears. Alec could hardly hold in a smile as she pulled her cloak close. Facing the door, she seemed anxious for Reams to open it and flee before Christian remarked on anything else.

"We r-r-really must go," she said, tugging on Alec's arm.

He humored her and let her lead him to the carriage, his mother close behind.

"We'll see you both at the ball," Alice called from the front steps.

"Thank you for a wonderful afternoon," Isabella called as she waited to be handed into the carriage. "I should like to come again."

"Please do." Alice waited until the carriage door shut before she went back inside.

She seemed like a good sort, Alec thought, and she'd obviously been a true friend to Elizabeth. That alone endeared her to him.

Isabella smoothed her skirts and settled into her seat. "The marquess and his wife are quite amiable, and their charity work for the veterans so admirable. I wonder, perhaps, if we might knit scarves or socks for the veterans, especially with cold weather coming. I'm sure some would have a need."

"What a s-splendid idea! We should s-speak to Alice about that at the b-ball this evening." Elizabeth touched her hand to her throat. "You'll b-be there, won't you?"

"Yes, I'm planning to attend." Isabella adjusted her skirts and crossed her ankles in front of her. "You'll be my escort, won't you, son?"

Alec patted his mother's arm. "Of course." He leaned in. "I'd like to discuss with Christian what measures have been taken for those veterans who aren't members of his club. Perhaps look into sheltering them or training them for a position so they can find work."

"If there isn't something already in place, perhaps Christian w-would want to p-partner with us to do something about that." Elizabeth clasped her hands together. "We c-could truly m-make a difference in the lives of these men and their families."

Alec liked the word *partnership* when it came from Elizabeth's lips and included him. "I would be honored to partner in such an endeavor."

The carriage stopped in front of Suffield House, and Alec moved forward in his seat so he could exit first. "Until this evening, then, my lady." He reached for her hand and kissed her gloved knuckles.

Elizabeth let him hold her hand just a moment too long before slowly drawing away. "I'll hold a spot for you on my dance card, my lord," she said, lowering her eyelashes.

"It's the thing I'm looking forward to most, lass." Alec couldn't take his eyes off of her, even when the door opened and the footman put down the steps.

He grinned at her blush, then exited the carriage, holding out his hand to help his mother down. As they walked up the steps to Suffield House together, he turned to watch Elizabeth's carriage until it turned a corner. A feeling of contentment washed over him. He would never have imagined thinking that London would ever feel familiar, but he'd felt like he belonged here today. He'd enjoyed Elizabeth's friends and seeing her so happy. He esteemed Elizabeth greatly, and from her words and actions, she seemed to hold him in the same regard. He couldn't keep his smile from growing even wider at the thought. His heart was light and if he could, he would shout his exhilaration from the rooftops.

Life was grand, indeed.

CHAPTER 8

*E*lizabeth was humming when she entered the house and gave her cloak, hat, and gloves to the butler. The afternoon with Alec had been perfect. His tender touches had made her heart flutter, and he'd genuinely seemed to like Alice. More than that, Alice had liked him, too. Her character judgment had always been dependable and Elizabeth was glad Alec had seemed to meet with Alice's approval.

"There you are." Her father's stern voice made her jump. She turned to face him.

"H-hello, Father." Elizabeth swallowed hard. He looked angry. Had something happened? She hadn't thought she was late and couldn't think of any reason her father would be upset with her.

"Where have you been?" He looked first at Elizabeth, but before she could reply, he turned to Tess. "You may address my questions, as I haven't the patience for my daughter today."

Elizabeth's ears turned red at the insult. She should be used to his unpleasantness by now, but somehow it still pricked her. At Tess's worried look, she gave her a slight nod.

Tess took a breath. "Your Grace, we were at the Veterans Club with the Marquess and Marchioness of Wolverton."

"My daughter was at a club?" Her father frowned. "Why would women be at a club? Surely there are better uses for your time."

"It's for veterans, my lord," Tess said. "Lady Elizabeth was doing her charitable duty."

"Who else went along on this outing?" Her father's eyes narrowed when he looked at her. "Did you take Lord Lindley along, by chance?"

"No, Your Grace. We were accompanied by the Earl of Suffield and his mother." Tess gave her an apologetic look. Elizabeth lifted a shoulder. She wouldn't have expected Tess to lie. And there was nothing wrong with Alec and Isabella accompanying them.

"The Scot." Her father's eyes turned as hard as flint. "You are supposed to be acquainting yourself with your betrothed, not frequenting a club." His voice was low and derisive. "Even in the name of charity work, I don't want my daughter in the company of any man that isn't Lord Lindley. Do I make myself clear?"

Elizabeth could hardly hide her dismay. "B-but, Father, Lord Suffield is an earl and perfectly r-respectable," she started, but he cut her off with a slice of his hand through the air.

"Be quiet, girl. I can't abide your tangle tongue today, but you will listen to what I have to say." He drew closer to her, and it took all the courage Elizabeth had to stand her ground and not step back. She lifted her chin, drawing a wall around her heart that his incivility couldn't penetrate. His next words would not hurt her, no matter what they might be.

He leaned even closer until she could smell the fish on his breath that he must have had for luncheon. She took a shallow breath and stared at his cravat pin while he spoke. "You will focus on your intended at the Berwick ball tonight. You will dance a waltz and the supper dance with him. Smile and simper and show him you will be a docile and obedient wife. If you do not, I will announce your betrothal at the ball tonight, get a special license, and have you married and off my hands before the week is out." He pointed his index finger in her face to emphasize his point, then pivoted on his foot and marched down the hall.

Elizabeth stared after him, his words hitting like stones and stealing her breath. Tears pricked her throat, but she swallowed them back. He couldn't wait to see her gone from his house. The thought was like lead in her middle. She'd always known he didn't care for her, but she hadn't realized how truly impatient he was to have her out of his sight. His ultimatum echoed in her ears. She'd promised to dance with Alec at the ball and had been looking forward to it. What could she do?

"C-come along, Tess," she finally said as they slowly climbed the stairs to her bedchamber. Her feet felt as heavy as her heart.

Once inside, she immediately went to her wingback chair near the hearth and picked up her sketchbook from the seat. Holding it close, she sat down and shut her eyes, trying to get back her happy feelings from earlier in the day. Scenes from the afternoon flitted through her mind like tiny diamonds in the darkness her father had created. Elizabeth focused on the memory of Alec's face when he kissed her hand, the green of his eyes capturing her in their depths. His hearty laugh when he was speaking with the veterans. His care for his mother. Oh, he was wonderful in every way. What was she going to tell him?

"I'll go air out your ball gown, my lady," Tess said, as she moved toward the other room, where the wardrobe was located.

Elizabeth was glad to be left alone for a moment. Opening her sketchbook, she found the one of Alec she'd been working on since she met him on the street. That moment seemed so long ago now, though it hadn't been. Today, she was going to start a new portrait of him. A laughing Alec, his eyes crinkled and his mouth smiling wide. He was the bright spot she needed in her life right now.

"We should dress you, my lady, so we have time for your hair," Tess said softly, coming to her side.

Elizabeth looked at her maid. "I know. I'm m-merely d-delaying the inevitable."

Tess gave her a sympathetic nod, and they moved into the bedchamber. Her deep green gown, nearly the same color as Alec's eyes, was laid out on the bed. It was one of her favorites and had always made her feel pretty. As he did.

After Tess had helped her change, Elizabeth moved to the dressing table so the maid could start on her hair.

With only one side curled, her bedchamber door opened, and her mother glided into the room. She was dressed in her blue silk with the Barrington family's diamond jewels at her throat and ears. She stood and watched Tess work for a moment.

"Your father is in a foul mood today." Her mother clasped her hands in front of her.

Well, at least Elizabeth wasn't the only one to notice it. "Y-yes," she said, looking at her mother in the mirror.

"It would help greatly if you would do as he asks." Her mother's glance flicked to Tess. "Leave us. I must speak with my daughter."

Tess curtsied and left the room. Elizabeth turned in her chair and faced her mother. "H-he has asked m-me to be all that is k-kind and attentive to Lord Lindley this evening. Or else he will have me m-married to him by special l-license before Sunday." Where did her mother stand? Could she be an ally with the rest of Elizabeth's life and happiness on the line?

"Yes, he mentioned that." Her mother pulled a highback chair closer and sat down with a sigh. "I failed in my duty when I wasn't able to provide your father with an heir, and he's never forgiven me. Had your two brothers lived, they would have brought honor to both me and your father." The duchess picked at her skirt, a delicate crease on her forehead.

"H-he's never wanted me." Elizabeth had known it, but never voiced it until today.

Her mother looked up at her with sad eyes. "He wanted a son, yes, or a daughter who was whole and could make an advantageous match."

"I am whole." Elizabeth said the words slowly and was proud they came out clear.

"You know what I mean," her mother said with a wave of her hand. "Lord Lindley's father and yours have come to a beneficial agreement for both of our families, and our children being married is part of the bargain. You will help our family's status by doing your duty."

Elizabeth could hardly comprehend what her mother was saying. "A-am I n-nothing more than a f-financial transaction?" The tears were threatening again. "He w-would marry me to a m-man who disrespects me and openly admits h-he just wants my d-dowry?"

"Most marriages are financial transactions. Your father and I have learned to live together and do our duty. You will do the same." She stood. "I want you to look your best tonight."

"Mother, what if there w-were another s-suitor?" Elizabeth needed a tiny shred of hope that her life would amount to more than doing her duty as Lindley's wife. "Would father c-consider it?"

"I'm sure your father would consider every offer before he decided what's best for you." Her mother gave her a small smile. "But be sweet and biddable tonight. For your father's sake."

Elizabeth bowed her head. She would do what was asked, but not for her father's sake. If her father thought she'd agreed to his demands, perhaps he wouldn't watch her as closely than he otherwise would. She needed an opportunity to tell Alec what was afoot and urge him to speak to her father with all possible haste.

"The carriage will be ready in an hour's time. Don't be late," her mother said before she went to the door and disappeared into the hallway.

Tess came back in, and Elizabeth turned back to the dressing table mirror. "I'd like to wear my grandmother's m-moonstone and p-pearl jewelry," Elizabeth told her. "And maybe have a few p-pearls in my hair."

Her grandmother had been a formidable woman, and the moonstone and pearl set had been her favorite. She'd worn it often when she was alive and since Elizabeth needed a bit of fortitude tonight, perhaps wearing her jewelry would help.

While Tess worked so Elizabeth would look her best, Elizabeth thought about how she could still give her promised dance to Alec. Perhaps while they danced she could tell him of the urgency to speak to her father about his suit. Yes, as soon as the duke had retired to the card room, she would find Alec.

Remembering his tender look as he'd kissed her knuckles in farewell brought a flush to her cheeks. Yes, she would see Alec tonight and he would help her out of this muddle with her father and Lord Lindley. Having Alec court her was everything her heart wished for, and he gave her hope that anything was possible.

She couldn't wait to see him.

CHAPTER 9

*I*t felt like days since Alec had left Elizabeth's side, though it had only been a handful of hours. The glittering jewels, beautiful gowns, and jaw-dropping mounds of flowers and candles that draped every surface of the Berwick home all faded into the background as he searched the ballroom. So far, he hadn't managed to locate Elizabeth.

He saw his mother in the corner with the Duchess of Huntingdon, no doubt speaking about Kitty and the duchess's search for a terrier of her own. The duchess had taken his mother under her wing, and Alec was glad to see her with a friend. Both women were talking animatedly and smiling, which always warmed his heart. Though he wouldn't dare interrupt their coze, he wouldn't have minded having his mother's help in searching for Elizabeth.

No, this was one undertaking he would have to attend to alone. And if the fates were smiling on him, he might have a bit of privacy with Elizabeth. If the moment was right, perhaps he would rally his courage enough to hold her hand and confess how she had wholly captured his heart with her determination and wit, her beauty and bravery. If only he could find her.

Dancing had already begun, but he didn't see her on the dance floor. Lindley had partnered with a young woman who thankfully wasn't Elizabeth. Alec watched for a moment as Lindley held the woman much too close and stole glances down her bodice each time he came within arm's reach. Alec hadn't thought it possible, but his disgust for the man increased. He didn't deserve to breathe the same air as Elizabeth, or any lady of breeding. If only Elizabeth's father could see that.

Turning away, he caught sight of a blonde head between two large potted plants. Smiling, he moved closer.

Elizabeth had taken shelter in one of the darker corners of the room, where the large potted trees shielded her. She was dressed in a deep-green gown that would make his favorite hills in Scotland pale in comparison. Pearls were scattered in her hair, winking at him, as if a beacon for him to go to her. His heart drummed a beat of happiness as he complied.

Alice stood next to her, and their heads were so close together, they didn't see him at first. When Elizabeth looked up and spied him, a smile briefly crossed her face before it was gone. Alice noticed Elizabeth's change in countenance and turned to see who had caused it, coming face-to-face with Alec.

He bowed over her hand. "My lady, how nice to see you again."

"My lord." She turned to Elizabeth and flipped open her fan. "Elizabeth, Alec, I must thank you both for your willingness to help at the Veterans Club this afternoon. It was so wonderful to see you both in a place that means so much to me. But I shan't keep you any longer, Elizabeth. Weren't you just saying you'd like to get some air on the terrace?"

Alice gave Alec a conspiratorial smile as she nudged Elizabeth.

Alec quirked a brow at her obvious matchmaking, but he wouldn't waste the opportunity.

"It would be my pleasure to escort you to the terrace," he said to Elizabeth, trying not to appear too eager.

Stepping closer, he longed to reach for the lone curl that had been left out of her complicated hairstyle. The curl hugged her collarbone and drew his eye to the moonstone and pearl necklace nestled there. Since moonstones were said to have calming powers, he fleetingly wondered if she'd been excited to being in his company again. He'd hardly been able to think of anything else. Was it her necklace keeping her calm and collected?

Winging his elbow out for her, he gave an encouraging smile. "My lady?"

Elizabeth hesitated and glanced back at the crowd before she took Alec's arm. Was she looking for Lindley? A trickle of unease went through him. She hadn't seemed happy to see him and hadn't spoken a word to him since his arrival. Something was wrong. Had he upset her? Or had Lindley? His grip on her arm tightened slightly as he led her outside to the balustrade at the edge of the terrace.

He wanted to stop and demand to know what had happened since they'd been apart, but he didn't want to frighten her, though his need to hold and comfort her was great. He drew her close, and her body trembled in his arms. "What's wrong, *mo chridhe?*" he whispered into her hair.

She turned her face into his lapel, her unhappiness finally coming to the surface. "I-I don't know how to tell you," she said, her voice so soft he had to bend to hear her words.

Alarm started to burrow its way into his heart. "Are you ill?" She shook her head. That left one option. Only Lindley could provoke this sort of reaction.

Alec stroked her back to comfort himself as well as her. "Has

Lindley done something to distress you?" He kept his voice level, wanting her to trust him and be reassured by his presence. "Whatever it is, let me help you."

She drew away and looked up at him, moonlight reflecting on her beautiful blue eyes, which saw straight into his soul. "I wish you could t-take me away from here."

"I can. If you wish it, we'll leave tonight. I'll carry you off like the barbaric Highlander I am." She didn't laugh at his jest. He touched her cheek. "Tell me." Fear at her reticence to confide in him was starting to overtake his concern, but he pushed it back.

Elizabeth took a deep breath. "My f-father has threatened to purchase a special license to marry me off before the w-week's end if I don't play the d-dutiful fiancée tonight by d-dancing attendance on Lindley."

Alec cursed softly under his breath. His beautiful Elizabeth anywhere near that cad was unthinkable. "What did you say?"

Elizabeth bit her lip, her eyes downcast. "What c-could I say?" She kept her eyes on her shoes and blushed adorably. "W-would you ask my father's permission to c-court me as soon as possible?"

Alec gently lifted her chin with one finger. "I'd gladly be on your doorstep at dawn tomorrow morning. Ye needn't worry about that. And once I have your father's permission, we'll make him see that I am the better match for you." He bent down and met her eyes. "Aye?"

"Aye." She gave him a sweet smile, but then shifted her eyes away from his. There was more to tell.

"What is it, lass? Ye can trust me." He slipped his arm around her shoulder and she put her head on his chest. Alec wished he could hold her like this for far longer than the few moments they had left together on the terrace.

"I'm afraid my f-father will choose Lindley b-because he's English," she said softly.

"I'll just have to use my Scottish charm on him," Alec said lightly, but she was right. Her father didn't seem to have any love for Scotsmen.

"I'm sure that w-would help." She relaxed and nestled closer. Alec let the tension seep out of him as well. He squeezed her shoulder in reassurance.

They stayed close together, looking up at the stars until he felt her shiver. They needed to go back inside. "I d-don't want to spend the evening with Lindley, but I'm afraid if I d-disobey his wishes, my father will make good on his threat and announce our betrothal before s-supper."

Her words were barely more than a whisper on the breeze, but each syllable was a knife to his heart. "I don't want him anywhere near you."

"He threatened to say that I was ruined if I didn't go along with the courtship." The words came out in a rush, as if they were too horrible to be spoken.

Alec cursed softly under his breath. "When?"

"The day I visited your mother in her garden. After Lindley called, my mother excused herself to discuss the evening meal with Cook." She looked up at him, her eyes wide and afraid. Alec pulled her close wanting to give her some of his warmth and strength.

"She left you alone with him." The man seemed to have worked some kind of sorcery on her parents. Alec's fists clenched as Elizabeth's words echoed in his mind. "And I'll wager he threatened you the moment she gained the hall."

Lindley had gone too far. Alec turned to walk back into the ballroom and show the man what he thought of his cowardly tactics, but Elizabeth anticipated his reaction and held him back.

"He's powerful, Alec. I have no d-doubt he would f-follow through on his th-threat and start rumors about you and your m-mother. I d-don't want to see either of you h-hurt." Her stammer was noticeably increasing, testifying to her distress. Alec let out a sigh.

"I can't let him get away with this," he said, covering her hand with his, feeling her fluttering pulse in her wrist. "I care not what he says. I won't have him hurting anyone I care about." He stared into the depths of her clear blue eyes, his protective instincts rushing forward, making him want to wrap her in his arms and never let go.

"I don't w-want you hurt in any way." She blinked back tears. "And the only w-way to m-make sure of that is to g-go along with his wishes and my father's."

"Over my dead body," Alec growled. "We just need a little more time. Why don't ye tell yer ma that ye feel a megrim coming on and need to go home immediately. Then, I'll make an appointment with yer father first thing in the morning."

He smoothed her cheek with his thumb, surprised at the depth of his feelings. His care for Elizabeth overwhelmed him. Could he possibly love someone in so short a time? Bending, he kissed her lightly on the cheek. "Once I convince your father of the benefits of our courtship, I'll take care of Lindley." Though Alec would have to be at his most persuasive when he talked to the duke, since her father hadn't exactly been welcoming to him thus far.

"No," she said with a small shake of her head. "Once my f-father agrees, I never want to have any d-dealings with Lindley ever again. F-For either of us."

Her confidence buoyed him. Surely her father would see that a love match would be advantageous for his daughter and that she would be happy as Alec's wife.

"That suits me just fine." He held her hand over his heart. "As soon as we're married, perhaps we can retire to the country and ride across the fields, shouting at the sky until we're hoarse."

She grinned, the worry in her eyes fading slightly. "That s-sounds like heaven."

He pulled her near once more and, resting his chin on her head, wished he could protect her and keep her safe from the likes of Lindley. Soon. But right now her mother would probably be looking for her, and they needed to return to the ball.

"Are we agreed, then?" he asked softly. "You'll go home and remain out of harm's way until I can work everything out with yer father?"

"Agreed." She took a fortifying breath. "I h-hope he listens. My f-father has a way of talking over people."

"I'll make him listen," Alec promised. "You were meant to be mine, *mo chridhe*."

She gave him a shy smile, straightening his cravat. "What d-does *mo chridhe* mean?"

"I'll tell you someday," he whispered, before he kissed her brow. "But tonight, I'd like to show you."

Cradling her face, he bent down and claimed her mouth. He took his time, exploring her lips, letting his hand caress her nape. She was so soft and sweet. Deepening the kiss, he pressed her close to him, and she wrapped her arms around his neck. She was his perfect fit, the love he'd been waiting for.

His heart was pounding, and her breaths were uneven as he reluctantly broke off the kiss. He leaned his forehead against hers. "Tomorrow can't come soon enough," he said as he exhaled.

She shivered and whispered, "I'll be w-waiting for you."

With one last caress of her delicate cheek, they went back inside. Alice spied their entrance and motioned to the left. Elizabeth's mother was on tiptoe, obviously searching for her, but hadn't seen them yet.

"Slip into the crowd," Alec murmured.

Elizabeth squeezed his arm as she moved away. His feet automatically followed, as if his body couldn't bear to be parted from her for even a moment, but he forced himself back. He needed to keep his distance for now, but only until he'd spoken to her father. Then, hopefully, his suit would be accepted and this madness with Lindley would be nothing more than a bad memory. He watched her speak with her mother, touching her temples. Her mother frowned and shook her head, but after more pleading on Elizabeth's part, they both moved toward the entrance.

Good.

They motioned to two footmen, and it was obvious they were calling for the duke and their carriage. Out of the corner of his eye, he saw Lindley watching the two women, but he didn't approach.

One part of Alec wanted to call the man out, but that would serve no purpose. Though Alec was a crack shot, it would mortify his mother if he participated in a duel and possibly confirm any rumors of his "savage" tendencies because of his Scottish heritage —the very thing Lindley wanted. No, better to do things properly, by appealing to Elizabeth's father. Holding back took all his self-control, though. Lindley deserved a good thrashing, but this wasn't the time for it.

When Elizabeth and her mother had safely departed in their carriage, he crossed the ballroom in search of his own mother. He considered carefully what he would say to Elizabeth's father in the morning, but needed his mother's counsel. If anyone knew how to deal with the peculiarities of an English nobleman and could tutor him on the best approach, she could.

The gauntlet had been thrown, and he couldn't afford any errors in planning how to obtain her father's permission for Alec to win Elizabeth's hand.

CHAPTER 10

*A*fter Elizabeth came home, she went directly to her room on the pretense of her head aching. But once inside, she leaned against the door, her lips curved in a smile, reliving the best part of the night. Alec had kissed her. She hugged herself, unable to contain the happiness inside as she twirled around the room. Though her head urged her to be careful, her heart was ready to take the leap into the unknown with Alec by her side.

Tess came in and helped her into a nightdress before retiring, but energy hummed through Elizabeth. She didn't try to sleep. Instead, she went to her desk, where she got out her sketchbook and pencils. Turning to Alec's portrait, which she'd never finished, she sat down and began to work. His jaw took shape, and she added a brush of stubble on it, recalling how it had felt under her fingers. His dark hair was next, framing the eyes she could easily get lost in. She worked hard to get each feature just right, his face coming alive on the page.

When the sun started to peek over the horizon, she rolled her shoulders and put her pencil down. Holding up the page, she stared at her drawing. It was one of the best portraits she'd ever done, as if her feelings for him had guided the pencil and allowed her to capture the way he looked at her—with a hint of wonder, mixed with admiration and maybe even love. Through his eyes, she felt treasured and worthwhile.

Letting out a breath, she carefully placed the portrait on her desk and lay down on the bed. Covering up, she closed her eyes and fell asleep to dreams of sweet kisses and whispered words.

When she woke, the sun was already streaming into her room, and Tess was knocking on the door. "C-Come in," Elizabeth called, her voice still husky from sleep.

Tess hurried into the room with a worried look in her eyes. "My lady, your father is asking for you to come to his study immediately."

Had she missed Alec's visit? "Has anyone c-come to c-call this morning?" Elizabeth asked, excitement rushing over her. He did say he would come early.

"Yes, my lady. The Earl of Suffield was here." Tess went to the wardrobe and pulled out a day gown.

Elizabeth was already taking out her night braid. The interview must already be over. That had to be what her father wanted to speak with her about. A tremor of anxiety chilled her, and she took her wrap from the chair and pulled it over her shoulders.

Tess picked up the hairbrush and promptly tried to tame Elizabeth's hair. Watching her in the mirror, it was hard to see Tess's worried expression and not feel that emotion herself.

"We need to hurry." Elizabeth wished she were already presentable or didn't need to take time on her appearance. Her future had been decided, and she needed to know the outcome.

It took longer than Elizabeth would have liked to dress and fix her hair, but the moment she was ready, she took a deep breath and walked sedately down the stairs to her father's office. Her governess had drilled into her that a lady never runs, but right now, she wanted to race into her father's study and hear the words she'd dreamed of---that he'd given his permission for Alec to formally court her.

The closer she got to the study, however, the more a sense of foreboding shadowed her steps. It would be customary for Alec to stay and speak to her. Why hadn't he? Stopping outside the study door, she put her hand to her middle. Maybe he'd been told she was still abed. There had to be an explanation.

Don't panic.

After her quick knock, her father called out a firm, "Come in."

She opened the door to find her father behind his desk as always, but her mother was in an armchair near the door. That was unusual. Her parents were rarely in the same room together. Her apprehension ratcheted up a notch.

Elizabeth swallowed. "Y-You wanted to s-s-see me?" Curse her stutter. *Stay calm,* she told herself.

"The Earl of Suffield was here this morning," her father said, barely glancing at her, getting right to the point. "He asked my permission to court you."

Elizabeth stood there, her hands clenched together. This was the moment she'd been waiting for her entire life—to have a suitor she could respect and love—but her parents weren't smiling, and her mother wouldn't look at her. "Y-Yes?"

Please see my heart. See that Alec is what's best for me.

But her hope waned with the resolute look on her parents' faces. Her father glanced at her mother, giving her a slight nod. Apparently, he didn't wish to say the words himself and was making her mother do it, which meant he wanted to soften the blow. Dread pooled in Elizabeth's chest.

Her mother cleared her throat. "Elizabeth, your father and I feel that with the earl being raised in Scotland . . ." She trailed off but was bolstered after a pointed glance from her husband. "We think you are just too different for each other and won't suit."

Her father pinched the bridge of his nose. "What she's trying to say is that I turned him down," he said bluntly. "I have an agreement with Lord Lindley's father, and you are promised to his son. He offers the right connections and a proper bloodline, so I've decided it's best for you to be settled right away and put away any more childish notions of love and marriage. You will do your duty in this matter."

Her mother stood and came around to her side. She gave a reassuring pat to her arm. "In time, you will see the wisdom of this decision," she told Elizabeth. "When you are married to Lord Lindley with your own household and responsibilities, you'll look back with no regrets."

Elizabeth felt numb as tears streamed down her face. They'd turned Alec away. The man she'd given her heart to had been dismissed because he was too different, but those very differences were what drew him to her.

Shock, anger, and disappointment spiraled into a ball of emotion that lodged in Elizabeth's throat. "N-N-No," she said, her voice coming out as a mere squeak. "I w-w-won't. A-A-Alec is w-w-wonderful, and I-I—"

Her father cut her off. "This isn't a topic for debate. You are the only daughter of the Duke of Barrington, and as the bearer of that title, it is my duty to ensure that your future is secure with a suitable husband."

"I-I am of age. You c-cannot force m-me." She clenched her hands and took a breath, fighting for calm. "I r-refuse to m-marry Lord L-Lindley. He's a c-cad."

"You will do what I say." Her father's face was growing red. "Once you are married to Lord Lindley, I will have a powerful ally in his father." He came around the desk and stood in front of her.

It took all the courage Elizabeth had to meet his hard gaze. "You will obey me."

"Are you s-selling me to Lindley f-for his father's g-goodwill?" Anger rushed through her veins. "Did you b-bargain for m-me like a common street vendor s-selling his wares?"

Her father stinging slap caught her by surprise as her head snapped to the side. "I could hardly *give* you away," he seethed, taking her by the arm. "I have no heir, only a dim-witted daughter. You're lucky I didn't send you to an asylum!" His voice steadily rose until he was shouting in her ear. His grip on her arm was like iron as he yanked open the door and thrust her through. "You have been nothing but a stain on the Barrington name, and you will finally do something beneficial with your wretched existence."

Elizabeth tried to pull away, but he only squeezed tighter as he hauled her up the stairs and down the hall to her bedchamber. Throwing open her door, he threw her in and she stumbled and fell to the floor. He stood over her, breathing hard. "You will stay in this room until you are ready to obey and bring honor to your family."

Tess appeared in the doorway and he turned on her. "You are not allowed to bring her food or water without my permission, do you understand?" Tess looked at him wide-eyed, then down at Elizabeth. "My lord . . ."

He cut her off. "If I find that you've disobeyed me, you will be let go without a character."

With that, he turned on his heel and escorted Tess into the hallway, before he slammed the door shut. Elizabeth jumped at the sound, but when she heard a key in the lock, she quickly got to her feet. Was he really making her a prisoner? She tried the door handle, and it didn't budge. She was locked inside.

What was she going to do now?

As if in a daze, she walked to the window and drew back the

curtains. She'd had such hopes for today. Leaning her head against the glass, she closed her eyes, still feeling as though she'd been thrown from her horse and the wind knocked out of her. But what had she expected? Her father had long been set on Lindley, apparently for the influence he would have with Lindley's father. Lindley had offered to take a *mute*, and his wager had borne fruit. She was to be his prize, willing or not.

Walking over to her desk, she picked up Alec's portrait. His eyes stared back at her, kind and full of love. A picture was all she would ever have of him now, and she wouldn't be allowed to keep it after she married Lindley.

The tears came faster, but Elizabeth let them come. It was over. She'd lost at love. Her steps were slow as she moved to the fireplace, hugging the picture tight to her chest. Her heart was breaking into a million pieces, but she wouldn't let them take anything else from her.

She carefully put his portrait into the fire and watched it slowly disappear. The edges burned first, then the middle, twisting as the flames eagerly devoured the paper. Watching the picture burn to ashes, Elizabeth knew in that moment her dreams had gone with it. Curling up in her bed, she cried for what might have been until there were no more tears left.

CHAPTER 11

*A*lec couldn't go home after his interview with the Duke of Barrington. He walked the streets, letting anger fuel his steps. He found himself traipsing through Hyde Park and ended up near the exact spot where he'd met Elizabeth and that boor Lindley in the park. It was where he'd held her in his arms for the first time. Taking a breath, he let the memory of her courage wash over him from that day. She had a warrior spirit inside her, and Alec was glad since Elizabeth would need it. Her quest for freedom wouldn't be easily won.

It was early morning yet, so the only other people in the park were nursemaids and their charges. Alec lingered a little, watching the little lads and lassies running about, laughing and giggling. One little blonde girl didn't participate in the games and sat primly on a bench watching the other children. Her solemn expression matched her nursemaid's, yet he could see the longing in her eyes to get down and run. She reminded him of Elizabeth. That little girl should be laughing and playing, secure in the knowledge she was loved and treasured---that getting her pinafore dirty was of no consequence. Was that how Elizabeth had been raised? To think more of her appearance and behavior than being free to run and play? Most likely. The thought added a little more fuel to his anger.

Alec walked on, letting the trees above and dirt beneath his feet soothe his temper. How he wished he were at home in Scotland or on Colin's estate where they would ride horses' neck for nothing across the moors until it felt like they were flying. But he was in England, losing his heart to an English lass whose father didn't care if his daughter ever experienced love in a marriage.

With a sigh, he finally turned for home. When he walked through the front door, his mother met him there, anxiously wringing her hands. She barely waited for him to hand his coat to Banks before she threw her arms around him.

"Where have you been? I've been so worried." She stepped back, her brows drawing together in concern. "From the look on your face, I gather your interview with the duke didn't go well?"

Alec took a breath, then steered her into the parlor and shut the door. "He hardly let me get a word in edgewise. Said my Scottish upbringing would be a detriment to a marriage with a duke's daughter and that we wouldn't suit. Apparently, Lindley's pure English heritage is more significant than anything I could offer." He clenched his fists as he remembered the slight curl to the duke's lips as he spoke, as if even saying *Scotland* was beneath him.

His mother put her hand on her chest. "What did you say to that?"

"That I could make his daughter happy. That she would have love and respect as the Countess of Suffield." Alec remembered how the duke had waved his declaration away, as if it didn't signify in the least. "He wouldn't listen to a word I said. Once he'd rejected me, that was that. He couldn't be bothered with objections."

Or letting him see Elizabeth. Alec had wanted to explain to her, but the duke had refused, saying it was best if Alec didn't see Elizabeth again. Even thinking those words made his ribcage squeeze. She was meant to be with him. He was sure of it.

His mother moved toward the settee and sank down, patting the seat beside her. Alec sat, though his body wanted to pace with energy.

She inhaled, then raised her face to meet his gaze. "Your situation reminds me a bit of what your father and I went through. When I first met him, there was something between us from the beginning. Being with him made me happier than I'd ever been and I felt as if he was the other half of me. We were better when we were together. My father wasn't pleased, to say the least, but he could see that I was in love and gave his permission for the marriage. But when your father announced our betrothal to his family, they were appalled and threatened to disown him if he went through with the marriage."

Alec started in surprise. He'd only heard that his father had been estranged from his family—never that his marriage had been the cause. His mother's eyes dropped to her hands folded in her lap. Did she still find it hurtful to speak about? "Was their only objection that you were Scottish?"

She looked up at him, her expression sad. "Yes. Some in England will never have any love for Scots." With a sigh, she leaned in and rested her head on his shoulder. "I'd hoped that perhaps some attitudes had changed since I was last in London, but it appears not. I'm sorry, son. I wish it weren't so."

They both stared at the fire in the grate for a moment, each lost in their own thoughts. "Was Da torn between you and his family?" Alec asked softly. Would an attachment to Alec have forced Elizabeth to make a similar choice?

"No. We loved each other so much it wasn't even a question. We went ahead with our marriage plans, eventually settling in

Scotland, and we never looked back. Both of us assumed his father had followed through on his threat to disown your da, which is why it was such a surprise when the earldom fell to you."

She straightened and turned slightly to face him. "I suppose what I'm trying to say is that, no matter the obstacles in front of you, if you truly love Lady Elizabeth, then she's worth fighting for, no matter what anyone else thinks."

She was right, but how could he prevail against Elizabeth's father? From their discussion this morning, the settlements were all but signed. So, though he wanted to fight for her, his efforts might not matter.

"I'm not sure what to do right now, Ma. I might blow retreat for today, so I can fall back and make a plan." He patted his mother's knee, then kissed her cheek. "I'd best be getting some estate business taken care of that I've been neglecting, though I'm glad you're willing to share your thoughts with me. There are difficult decisions ahead and your wisdom is invaluable to me."

She clasped her hands together and he could feel her eyes on him as he left. Rubbing a hand over his jaw, he walked into his office and shut the door. Sinking down into the chair behind the desk, he looked morosely at the tray of shortbread Mrs. Jennings had put there. The memory of Elizabeth's happiness when she'd "tested" the treat in the garden popped into his head. The idea of never seeing her again was one he didn't care to think about. Perhaps he could still see her at society functions. She might need a friend.

Alec shook his head. No, she would soon be wed to Lindley if her father had his way and it would be torture to see her on that dunderheid's arm, knowing she was miserable. Alec closed his eyes and clenched his fists. He felt so helpless.

Mayhap he needed to leave London. He could go to Lanford Park and look at the thoroughbred there, see if Ares might be a fit for the horses he and Colin had purchased for breeding. But how could he leave Elizabeth when she might need him? There were no answers.

He took a piece of shortbread and ate it in one bite as his mind tried to find a solution to his problem. There had to be another way to convince her father to accept his suit and show him that Alec was worthy of his daughter. Perhaps he should have reminded the duke that Alec was the nephew of the current Duke of Argyll as well as an English earl. He owned several estates and was in sound financial shape. He'd formed an acquaintance with the Marquess and Marchioness of Wolverton. What connections would appeal to the Duke of Barrington?

Alec quickly ate two more pieces of shortbread and found his mood improving. He had connections and some standing. Surely, the duke would take that into account before he consigned Elizabeth to Lindley's cold-blooded care. Alec had to try and talk to the duke again.

For Elizabeth's sake and his own, he wasn't going to give up just yet.

CHAPTER 12

The first day Elizabeth was confined to her room wasn't terrible. She kept herself busy by catching up on her correspondence to Alice. She worked on some preliminary sketches of Kitty to see what pose might show off the little dog's best attributes. She took a nap. But by evening, her stomach growled with hunger and her throat was parched. Surely Father didn't mean to starve her. But when night came and there was no food tray and a cold hearth, Elizabeth knew her father was far more cruel than she had imagined.

Elizabeth tugged on the bell pull. Tess would be allowed to help her out of her dress, at least. The duke couldn't begrudge her that small comfort. But after an hour, Elizabeth gave up. No one was coming. After taking the pins out of her hair, Elizabeth brushed the long strands and plaited it. At least she could keep some of her routines in place.

When night came she lay on her bed, trying not to think about the stays digging into her sides. She'd never slept in her gown before. It wasn't an experience she wanted to repeat. Uncomfortable and cold,

Elizabeth stared up at the canopy of her bed, and silent tears rolled down her cheeks. How could the situation have escalated so far? The meeting with her parents that morning went through her head again. Her father's anger had almost seemed to have a thread of desperation to it. Why did he need her married off to Lindley so quickly? Was the contract with Lindley's father for more than financial reasons? Something didn't feel right, but Elizabeth couldn't say what exactly.

Turning over, she tried to get as comfortable as she could and pulled the blanket over her. Thoughts of Alec crowded her mind the moment she closed her eyes. Would he notice her absence from the Grafton musicale this evening? She'd been hoping to converse with him or maybe even take a turn in the gardens. Oh, Alec. Elizabeth had never felt a pull as strong as this to any other person. She yearned for his company, especially now.

Had he been terribly hurt by her father turning down his suit? How she wished the morning's events had been different. If Alec had been accepted, perhaps she could have gone to the musicale on his arm. Sat with him. Laughed with him. Basked in his acceptance. But she would rather stay in a locked room forever than be forced to marry Lindley. A part of her was proud she'd defied her father's orders. This was her life, and she should have some say. But another part was frightened. Her stomach rumbled again in protest, and she covered it with her hand. How long could she stay strong?

As long as it takes, she told herself fiercely.

Her last candle guttered out and Elizabeth finally fell asleep and slept until the morning sunshine streamed into her room. The air was chill and Elizabeth was loath to leave the warmth of her bed. After lying there for a few more minutes, however, she stretched her arms and legs and then got up to take care of her morning ablutions. Her dress was wrinkled, and she couldn't do anything to her hair beyond brush it out and plait it once again, but even doing that helped her feel a bit better.

With another glance at the cold hearth, she shivered and went to the wardrobe to retrieve her favorite shawl. Curling up in her favorite chair, she pulled her sketchbook onto her lap. She flipped through some pages, trying desperately not to think of her hunger and thirst. There was nothing she could do but try to take her mind off of her circumstances, and the only activity that made the world and everything in it go away was drawing. So that's what she would do this morning.

When she'd found a blank page, she started to sketch a self-portrait. As the piece took shape, Elizabeth drew herself strong and confident. Her hands were on her hips as if daring anyone to come near. The image in her head being transferred to the page was exactly what she wished would have happened when she'd stood in front of her father yesterday morning. In her imagination, she could speak her mind freely and would tell her father without tears or anxiety that she would accept Alec's suit and end Lord Lindley's hopes. Her pencil carefully shaded her features and made the portrait come to life under her fingers.

Hours later, the weak autumn light coming in from the window let her know that it was probably close to teatime. She put her sketchbook aside and as she did so, the room seemed to tilt. With one hand on her head to help the dizziness and the other on her hollow-feeling stomach, she leaned back in her chair. Perhaps lying down would help. Carefully rising from the chair, she went back to the bed and had just laid down when she heard the key in the lock. Elizabeth sat up and was relieved to see Tess in the doorway with a tray in her hands.

"My lady," she said quietly, moving toward the bed. "I've brought you some meat and cheese, with a pot of tea."

Elizabeth's eyes welled with tears at the loyalty of her maid. "Thank you," she whispered.

She slowly moved to the chair near her bed, willing away the dizziness that still threatened. Tess set the tray down on the escritoire. "I brought extra so that you can eat a little now and some later, in case I can't come back for a while."

Elizabeth was having difficulty concentrating on Tess's words when her mouth was watering so. She put some of the cheese in her mouth and chewed as slowly as she could. The urge to eat it all as quickly as possible was hard to quash. "I'm b-beyond grateful for the tray, but you really shouldn't have, Tess," Elizabeth told her. "If m-my father f-finds out . . ."

Tess squared her shoulders. "Your mother has been begging your father to relent, and the entire household is praying he'll listen to her. We're all appalled at what's happening, my lady. It's just awful. I couldn't stand by any longer, knowing you were hungry." Tess sat down in the chair across from hers. "How are you faring?'

Elizabeth could barely contain her surprise at the news that her mother was advocating for her. Usually the duchess went along with any and all of her father's wishes. Elizabeth took a long sip of her tea, thankful it wasn't hot enough to burn her. "As w-well as I can be. I'll admit I w-was very glad to see you."

Tess shifted her weight in the chair. "I'm worried, my lady. Your father seems set on keeping you in here until you agree to the marriage. Will he tire of waiting for your consent and force you to bend to his will?"

Elizabeth bit her lip. "I hope h-he won't try. I'm of age, so he can't f-force me. I'll stay locked in my r-room for as long as I have to instead of m-marrying Lord Lindley. He has no honor."

"I agree, my lady. But what will you do if your father doesn't relent?"

"I don't know. I've thought of trying to get w-word to Alice. But what c-could she do? My f-father won't let me l-leave with her, I'm sure. And she's so newly married, I would h-hate to intrude." Elizabeth sighed and looked down at the tray. She had finished a quarter of the meat and cheese. She had to save some for later, but her stomach still wanted more. Maybe she'd take just a few more bites. "I appreciate you t-taking such a risk to bring me f-food, but you must leave before you're caught. I would never f-forgive myself if you were let go without a character."

"Should I help you out of your dress before I go?" Tess asked, looking at her with sympathy in her eyes. "It can't be comfortable to have to sleep in your stays."

Tears pricked her eyes. Last night hadn't been comfortable at all. "My father has said he will check on me today to see if my answer has changed. He will know if I'm wearing a different gown and that someone has helped me. I can't risk that he'll make good on his threat to let you go. But thank you."

"Perhaps I could just help you into some short stays, so you can take them on and off yourself? Then we can put the same gown on again, so your father won't know," the maid suggested.

That sounded divine. "Oh, yes, that's a b-brilliant idea."

She stood and let Tess help her remove her stays. When she had dressed again, she felt much more comfortable. "Thank you, Tess," she said, taking a deep breath for the first time in two days.

Tess curtsied. "I can't bear to think of you suffering, Lady Elizabeth."

Elizabeth's emotion came to the surface again and tears welled in her eyes. "Your loyalty and kindness mean so much to me. I n-never thought my father would go this far, but I'll not bend. He can keep me p-prisoner and starve me, but I'll not m-marry that horrid man, no matter what agreement he's m-made with Lindley's father." She angrily brushed a tear away. "Never."

"Very good, my lady." Tess curtsied and moved to the door. "I'll do my best to get some food and drink to you as often as I can. Don't forget to hide the tray so your father sees nothing amiss."

"I will, but you mustn't jeopardize yourself for me." Elizabeth shook her head. "I couldn't bear it if anything happened to you at my father's hand." Her own cheek still stung from yesterday's slap.

"I'll happily risk your father's wrath to make sure you eat, my lady." Tess stepped forward and gave Elizabeth a spontaneous hug before she stepped back. "You deserve so much more, Lady Elizabeth."

With that, she cracked open the door and peeked into the hall. With one last nod to Elizabeth, she was gone. Elizabeth waited until she heard the lock click in the door once more before she let the tears come. How many tears were left inside of her? She thought she'd cried them all out. But, oh, it did feel good to have someone that cared for her well-being.

Once she'd gotten control of herself, she sipped her tea. Her mood had already improved just by having some nourishment. Her will had found a little more strength to go on.

Shivering, Elizabeth pulled her shawl closer around her and stared at the cold hearth. She should have asked Tess to help her build a fire, since it wasn't something a duke's daughter learned in the schoolroom. She'd never even thought of how a fire was built before, but she really needed one now.

It can't be that hard, she told herself. Going to stand in front of the hearth, she looked at the tinderbox on the mantel and the available wood on the side. When she thought back, it seemed as if the maid laid down small sticks on top of some of the larger ones. Then she'd used the tinderbox to get a flame and light the wood. Elizabeth had never done more than ask for more coal to be added to a fire already burning, but it seemed logical that the coal would

116

be added after the wood fire was already burning well. That's what she would try first.

She put on her oldest gloves to protect her hands as much as possible, then assembled the medium-sized wood and smaller kindling sticks in what seemed to be the most advantageous burning positions. Taking the flint and the steel from the tinderbox, she knelt down in front of the wood and struck them together. Sparks were coming out and falling on the wood, but it wasn't catching fire. Frustrated, she struck the flint and steel harder, but nothing was working. What was she doing wrong?

The tinder. That's what she was missing. Looking in the tinderbox, she carefully took out some charred cloth. Putting it in one hand with the steel, she used her other to strike the flint against it. *Yes!* A spark lit on the tinder. Quickly putting it underneath some of the small sticks, Elizabeth watched the fire build as more kindling caught the flames. Soon, some of the medium sticks were burning. As the flames got larger, Elizabeth felt a surge of triumph.

She moved closer, the warmth of the fire washing over on the outside and a sense of accomplishment on the inside. When the fire was going strong, she added coal to the grate. Walking to the chair near the hearth she looked down at her blackened gloves. They were definitely unsalvageable but would do as fire-building gloves while she was in her room. Elizabeth sat down and smiled. She'd done it. By herself! That accomplishment was one she'd never have thought of if she hadn't been locked in here. She was getting stronger in spite of her father.

That was unexpected.

All of her life had been about following the rules, obeying her parents, being docile, learning deportment, so she could make an advantageous match. And none of that had helped her. Now was the time for her to really reflect on what she wanted and what she would be willing to do to get it.

She sat in the chair for a long while, enjoying the warmth. Reaching for the tray that Tess had brought earlier, she took a bit of the meat and cheese for her evening meal. As she ate, her thoughts turned to her current situation. She could try to escape, but she had few friends and nowhere to go. She didn't feel comfortable imposing upon Alice and her new husband. Her gaze rested on her sketchbook with her first attempt at drawing Alec staring back at her. It remained unfinished, but the eyes were true-to-life and held her spellbound.

Alec would help her. She had no doubt he would offer her sanctuary, but her father could be furious and might even call him out. She would never forgive herself if Alec were hurt because of her, especially knowing how lost Isabella would be without her son. No, she couldn't involve Alec. She had to find an alternate solution.

The sun had set long ago, and Elizabeth's eyes were drooping. Deciding she'd have plenty of time tomorrow to think on more solutions to her circumstance, she walked to the bed and lay down. She pulled the covers over her and closed her eyes, easily bringing Alec's face to mind, their introduction when Kitty had run away, and his gallantry in the park when Lindley had threatened her. Or their outing to the Veterans Club. She'd never forget the tingles that had zipped through her body at his touch. But her favorite memory of all was his kiss at the Berwick Ball. She touched her lips. He had been everything she'd dreamed of for her first kiss. Gentle, yet thrilling. Her heart had nearly pounded out of her chest, and she'd felt sweetly powerful when she noticed how uneven his breathing had been when he'd finally parted from her. She'd affected this handsome Highlander as much as he'd affected her, and that was a heady feeling.

She sighed and turned over, hugging her pillow to her. His green eyes were mesmerizing, and his strong arms made her feel so safe. How she wished she could feel his embrace just once more. But if her father had his way, she wouldn't be seeing Alec ever again. The thought was sobering.

For right now, sleep would take her soon and she would find freedom in her dreams---that Alec was courting her, kissing her hand, and calling her lass. With another sigh, she willed him to come to her and keep her company through the night.

Because with dreams like that, she wanted to stay asleep as long as possible.

CHAPTER 13

*A*lec scoured the ballroom for Elizabeth. He hadn't seen her at any society event for nearly a week, and this was the last ball before most families retired to the country for the holiday season. She wouldn't miss this one. Something was wrong. He could feel it in his bones.

He folded his arms and leaned against a column, watching the other couples dance a country reel. He should be out there with Elizabeth. Smiling and laughing with her. But her father had stomped on that dream like a pesky insect under his shoe. Alec had requested another audience with the duke, but received no response, the snub another insult added to the long list Alec had already been dealt. No, Alec wasn't good enough for an English duke's daughter. She was going to marry Lord Lindley, and that was that.

Even thinking about the duke's words made Alec's blood boil anew. The man was everything an English lord was purported to be---arrogant, entitled, and rude. He had no care for anyone else's feelings, even his own daughter's. No matter what Alec had said regarding Elizabeth, her father had brushed it aside. The decision had been made, and Alec couldn't do anything about it.

He'd hoped to see her at a society event so he could explain or at least say goodbye. He couldn't stay in London and watch her be married to Lindley. Surely she would understand. But he hadn't seen Elizabeth or Lindley since the day he'd met with her father, and that worried him.

Pinching the bridge of his nose, he took a breath, then approached his mother who sat in the corner tapping her feet to the music. When she saw Alec's face, she stood. "She's still not here?" she asked quietly.

Alec shook his head. "Would ye call on her, Ma? I want to reassure myself she's well before we retire to Lanford Park."

"Of course I will. I'll go as soon as I can tomorrow." She looked around as the couples finished the dance and began clearing the floor. "Would you like to leave now? I'm a little tired tonight."

Alec snorted. His mother had more stamina than a woman half her age. She wasn't tired; she was worried about him and it warmed his heart to see her love for him. "Aye, I'd best get you home, then."

He offered his arm and escorted her to the entrance to get to get her wrap and have the carriage brought around. The ride through the streets of London was quiet, and as they passed the Barrington townhouse, Alec's eyes were drawn to the windows, but all was dark. Was she inside? Had her father spirited her away? Where was Lindley? He couldn't wait for his mother to call on her and hopefully return with some answers.

He hardly got any sleep that night, all sorts of dire scenarios running through his head. He arose early and busied himself with making all the preparations to move the household to Lanford Park at the end of the month. He'd had his fill of London and wouldn't be sorry to leave it behind.

Finally, it was time for proper visiting hours. His mother came down the stairs looking elegant in her new day gown. Alec was glad she'd been able to find a *modiste* she liked and a new lady's maid that suited her. Forcing himself to relax, he took her pelisse from Banks and helped his mother put it on. "Thank you for doing this for me," he said softly.

She put her hand on his face. "I am concerned for her, too." Banks opened the door, and Isabella stepped out, her new maid trailing her.

Alec watched her go for a moment, then retreated to the parlor. He could hardly keep still. He paced from one corner to the other until he heard the front door open again. He glanced at the ormulu clock on the mantel. It had scarcely been a quarter of an hour. What had happened?

He strode quickly to the front entryway. "What's wrong?" he demanded as his mother removed her bonnet. "Why are you back so soon? Did you see her?"

"I didn't even make it past the butler," she said, shaking her head. "He barely opened the door and said that Lady Elizabeth is not receiving. I tried to ask him a question, but he just repeated what he'd already said and shut the door." Isabella handed Banks her bonnet. "I think you're right. Something is very wrong."

"I have to do something." But what? He paced in front of his mother. "Perhaps her friend Alice has heard from her. I should go to the Veterans Club and call on her or her husband there."

With a plan in mind, he wasted no time. He donned his hat and greatcoat and mounted his horse, anxious to get answers. He wished he could let his horse run through the streets, but traffic was heavy at this time of day, and he had to be patient. Finally, he made it to the club where a stable lad came out to lead his horse to the mews. Alec strode to the entrance and rapped. Hopefully Lady Alice or her husband were here or the servants would know how to find them. He had to know that Elizabeth was all right.

Reams opened the door and peered at him. Not many men were his height, but Reams looked him in the eye. "My lord," the butler intoned.

"I'm looking for the Lord Wolverton or his wife," Alec said. "Are either of them here?"

"They're both in the dining room, my lord." Reams moved aside. "If you'll follow me."

"I know the way." Alec couldn't wait. His patience was at an end. Reams didn't protest when he moved past him and took the stairs two at a time. Alec was glad. He didn't want to offend the man if he was going to spend time here in the future.

He walked quickly down the hall, then strode into the dining room and scanned the people inside. He saw Alice on the far side speaking to Christian, and he immediately went to their side.

He bowed before speaking. "Lady Wolverton, Lord Wolverton, I apologize for the interruption, but have either of you spoken to Lady Elizabeth recently? I haven't seen her for nearly a week, and I'm worried."

A shadow crossed Alice's face and she looked at Christian. "We were just discussing this very thing. Elizabeth is a faithful correspondent, but I haven't heard from her either. When I tried to call on her this morning, I was turned away and told she wasn't receiving. That has never happened before. But I'm not sure what to do. I can't force my way inside."

That's exactly what he wanted to do. "Do you think she's ill?" Though his greatest fear was much worse than that. If her father had followed through on his threat to obtain a special license, Elizabeth could already be married.

"She's got a healthy constitution," Alice said slowly. "But she could be, I suppose, and the household doesn't want it known."

Alec couldn't hold the words in any longer. "Do you think her father could have forced her to marry that bounder Lindley?"

Christian let out a breath. "That's what we're afraid of. I was about to check with some of my contacts to see if I could find any information."

Alec clenched his fist. He had no contacts here in London. There wasn't anything he could do. "Could you inform me the moment you learn anything?"

"Of course." Christian put his hand on Alec's shoulder. "I can see how concerned you are, but I'm sure she's fine."

He hoped so. But his gut was telling him otherwise. "Thank ye." He bowed to them both and took his leave. He had no choice but to return home and wait for news.

His ride to Suffield House was much less urgent than his ride to the Veterans Club had been. There was no need to rush. As he passed Elizabeth's house, the urge to stop and knock on the door himself was nearly overwhelming, but Lord Lindley was just leaving. He didn't look right or left as he descended the stairs, but quickly got into his waiting carriage and left.

Alec's jaw clenched. Had he been there to see Elizabeth? His horse slowed, as if the animal knew Alec wanted to watch Elizabeth's door for any more visitors. None came. What was going on? Was Lindley there to discuss wedding details?

Dismounting, he glanced once more toward Elizabeth's home while his horse was led away. Frowning, he went inside, determined to ask his mother's advice. He couldn't sit and wait for news. He had to find a way to see for himself that Elizabeth was hale and hearty in body, if not in spirit. Banks took his hat and coat.

"Where is my mother?" Alec asked the butler.

"In the blue drawing room, my lord." Banks bowed and held out his hand. "She's waiting for you."

He started down the hall, but paused at a muffled pounding on the front door. Banks opened it. "Yes?"

"I must see the earl," a feminine voice answered.

"I'll see if he's at home," Banks said and started to close the door, but Alec recognized that voice.

He definitely was at home for this visitor. He strode to Banks's side and opened the door wide. "Tess?" Elizabeth's maid stood before him, glancing behind her every few seconds.

"I must speak to you, my lord. It's urgent." She was wringing her hands, making Alec's stomach tighten with worry.

"Has something happened? Is Lady Elizabeth all right?" He ushered her inside, more questions and an extra dose of concern running through him when the maid didn't answer right away.

"No, she's definitely not all right." Tess swallowed and shifted her weight from foot to foot. "I can't bear to see her like this."

"What's happened?" Fear coursed through Alec's veins. Had her father hurt her? He let out a harsh breath. If he had, Alec would make sure he regretted his actions.

"Lady Elizabeth's father informed her five days ago that she was to marry Lord Lindley or be locked in her room. When she wouldn't relent, he called a doctor from an asylum to the house. He . . . he . . ." Tess let out a little sob. "He's been bleeding her ill humors with leeches to make her more biddable. And when she resisted, he tied her to the bed." Tess wiped a tear away and it took every ounce of self-control that Alec had not to go to Elizabeth this very instant.

"I fear she's been drugged. No one from the household is allowed to see her, but Cook called the doctor downstairs to instruct her on how he wanted a certain poultice prepared and I tried to sneak in. I've been bringing her food every day, but once the doctor arrived it was nearly impossible. The duke caught me just now, and I was removed from his employ. Rather forcefully."

Tess rubbed her arm and inhaled. "I didn't know what else to do. She needs you."

Blood roared through Alec's veins and his vision clouded, the edges red with his rage. He'd only ever felt this way once before, during the war when he'd wanted to avenge the deaths of his closest kinsmen. "You did the right thing in coming to me. Did he hurt ye?"

"Just a bruise, I'm sure. But you have to go to her." Tess rubbed her arms as if she were cold and needed the friction to warm herself. "I fear for her life."

Alec's mind was racing. The thought of Elizabeth tied to a bed and drugged or bled against her will made him want to hit something. Hard. He had to put his emotions aside and think of a plan. Not only because it was his duty as a gentleman to protect a lady, but because she was his match. He knew it in his bones.

"Does His Grace know you are here?" Alec was trying to form a plan in his mind. He had to get her out of there.

"No. I made sure I wasn't followed." Tess raised her chin. "I would do anything for my mistress. She's got a good heart and doesn't deserve this abuse. It's evil!"

Alec's heart was pounding through his veins and he took a breath. "I'm going to get her out of there. Today."

"Thank you, my lord. I knew you would help her." She bobbed her head. "Just . . . please hurry."

"I will. You're a good woman, Tess. Do you have somewhere to go until I can go to Lady Elizabeth and assure her safety?" Alec led her to the drawing room.

Alec's mother met them at the door. She looked between him and Tess. "What's happened?"

"I will take my leave, now, my lord. I'd like to arrive at my sister's home before dark. She's expecting me." Tess curtsied. "Thank you."

"Let me have the carriage brought around for you. It's the least I can do." Alec motioned toward Banks, who swiftly walked down the hall to see it done.

"I can't stop saying thank you, my lord." Tess sank into a curtsy. "I'm just so worried, but I knew she could depend on you."

"Banks will be back shortly with the carriage." He touched her shoulder. "Thank you for trusting me. I'll not let Elizabeth down."

Tess nodded. "I know you won't." Her eyes were filled with tears and she turned toward the front door to wait for Banks.

Alec took his mother's arm and escorted her further into the drawing room. He helped her sit, then took the seat beside her. He had to move quickly, but he needed his mother's support.

"Elizabeth's father is threatening her and hired a doctor from an asylum. She's being drugged and bled with leeches until she agrees to marry Lindley. I canna let that stand, Ma, ye ken that. 'Tis my duty to help her." Alec looked down at his ma. If he stepped in to rescue the lady, the *ton* would talk, and reputations for both them, and Elizabeth could be compromised. They couldn't undo such consequences. "I've tried to do things the English way, but I've been brushed aside."

"Aye," his mother agreed, putting her hand on his forearm. "You're a Highlander, and a lady needs your assistance. I'll stand behind ye, my son. Always."

Alec looked down at the woman who had given him life. She'd always supported him, no matter the cost to herself. She was courageous and kind, always thinking of others. Attempting to rescue Elizabeth would be risky, but he had to try and knew his mother would be right behind him if she could. "Perhaps it's time to show the duke what it truly means to be a Highlander. Our people have always fought for everything we have. I'll not be any different. And Ma, you'll need to pack a bag."

His mother's eyes were bright. "You've the right of it," she said proudly, patting his chest. "And I'll stand beside you. *Tha gaol agam ort.*"

He kissed her forehead. "I love you, too."

Alec stood and walked out of the sitting room and took the stairs two at a time to his room. He went to his trunk, opened it, and took out his kilt, belt and buckle, sporran, and hose. After laying them out, he began to dress and, for the first time since coming to England, felt like his true self. The feeling spurred him on. He was doing the right thing.

Once he was dressed from his shirt down to his kilt pin and flashes, he slipped his *sgian-dubh* knife in the top of his hose, the hilt peeking out. He hoped he wouldn't have to use it as a weapon, but he wanted to be prepared, just in case. Determination drove him out the front door and along the pavement to the Barrington home.

The butler opened the door but, after one look at Alec, tried to close it again. Alec stuck his shoe in the gap and braced his shoulder against the door. "I'm here to see Lady Elizabeth."

"She's indisposed," the butler said, gasping for breath. "You must leave."

Alec was tired of being told what he must do. "Elizabeth!" he shouted, walking toward the stairs and climbing them quickly. "Elizabeth, I've come for ye, lass." He stopped on the second landing and addressed a maid who was staring wide-eyed at him around a corner. "Where is Lady Elizabeth's chamber?"

She pointed down the hall. "Second door on your left," she managed to say.

Doors started opening and closing. Servants peeked out to look at him, but no one attempted to stop him. He stopped in front of Elizabeth's door and tried the handle. Locked. "Elizabeth, lass, it's Alec."

No answer.

Looking at the lock, he planted one heel on the floor and raised the other to the side of the lock and kicked. The wood easily splintered. With one last kick, the door gave way. Alec shoved through the door. "Elizabeth?"

She wasn't in the sitting room, but sketches adorned the mantel and most of the available furniture. She must have used all the paper in her book. He walked through to the bedchamber, where a small man stood to one side of the bed, holding a bloody bowl in his hands. "What is the meaning of this?" he demanded. "You can't just barge in here when I'm with my patient."

"Get away from her." Alec's voice was little more than a growl as he advanced into the room. Elizabeth looked so pale and small as she lay on the bed, one of her arms tied above her head, and the other stretched out. He could hardly hold back his roar of anger.

The doctor backed up into a corner, his eyes wide. Alec didn't spare him a glance. He had to free her. Taking out his *sgian dubh*, he cut her loose. Elizabeth didn't stir and that was cause for concern. Looking at the table next to the bed, he saw the dark brown bottle and could smell the sickly, sweet scent of laudanum. She'd been drugged.

"Elizabeth?" He brushed his fingers over her cheek and her eyelids fluttered open.

"Alec?" Her voice was raspy. "Oh, Alec. I knew you'd c-come."

"Aye." He could barely control the fury rushing over him at her condition. After he used one of the available bandages sitting on the night table to wrap around her forearm, he scooped her up, coverlet and all. Clenching his teeth at how light she felt, he gently eased her through the door and walked down the staircase.

The duke was waiting for him in the great hall. "What is the meaning of this?" he blustered. "Put my daughter down and leave my home this instant."

"We're both leaving." Alec shifted Elizabeth's weight in his arms. "And if your daughter weren't in need of medical attention at the moment, I would call you out for what you've done."

"She's been under a doctor's care for her condition," the duke snarled. "And she is none of your concern."

"You're nothing more than the worst sort of coward. Your daughter should be cherished and protected. Not drugged and threatened!" Alec bellowed. "Stand aside."

"If you abduct my daughter, there will be serious consequences for you. Do you want that? Does your mother want that?" The duke's eyes narrowed. "Aren't you worried that your mother won't be received in good society? If you don't put my daughter down now, that's exactly what will happen."

Elizabeth trembled, and her arms tightened around his neck. "N-no, please. I c-can't go b-back."

Alec glared down at the man. "There's one thing you should know about me," he said slowly. "Anyone who threatens my family deals with me. If you ever so much as mention my mother to anyone, you will regret ever knowing my name."

He drew Elizabeth closer before he turned and strode to the front door. Her father quickly pushed in front of them, stopping in front of the door and folding his arms.

"You're not leaving," he said, his face a mottled red. "She's mine."

"She belongs to no man. Now get out of my way." Alec's voice was low and menacing. He couldn't plant a facer on the duke and blacken his eyes without putting Elizabeth down. He wasn't about to do that, but he would do whatever it took to protect her.

"You have no authority here." Her father braced his feet and folded his arms. As if his puffed-up show of domination would stop anyone.

Alec shouldered his way past the smaller man, careful to keep Elizabeth safe in his arms. Her father stumbled back, but kept his feet. "Open the door," Alec ordered the butler. The man didn't even look at the duke, just did Alec's bidding.

"You'll pay for this, Suffield," the duke growled. "You have no idea what you've done."

"I've saved your daughter from the man who should have protected her." Alec said as they passed through the doorway, cradling her body close to his heart. Blood still pounded through his veins, giving him extra strength and making him feel as if he could carry Elizabeth all the way back to Scotland, if that was what would keep her safe. She was his priority, which meant getting her away from here. Now. She needed medical attention.

"My mother is waiting for us," he said softly in her ear.

She huddled into his chest, but didn't say anything. Alec would call a physician the moment they were safe at Suffield House. He heard a small sniff from her and looked down to see the silent tears rolling from her closed eyes. Was she in pain? Did she have an injury he couldn't see? His footsteps quickened. She had to be well.

He couldn't imagine his life without her in it.

"Dinna worry, *mo chride*. I'll take care of everything," he said softly and kissed her temple.

And he was determined to do just that.

CHAPTER 14

For the first time in nearly a week, Elizabeth felt safe. Alec's arms surrounded her, and she wanted to burrow into his neck and stay right where she was. She let out a sigh. She didn't know if she could have lasted much longer. She'd never been more frightened than when the doctor from the asylum had forced laudanum down her throat. When she'd awoken, she'd been tied to the bed, except for one arm that had been cut, preparing for the leeches.

"We'll have the ill humor out of your blood in no time," the doctor had said.

She'd cried and screamed, but he'd merely stuffed a rag in her mouth and gagged her. No one had been allowed in her room and Elizabeth had nearly lost hope she'd live through her "treatment." Her body had steadily weakened with each passing day. Now, in Alec's arms, her ear listening to the steady beat of his heart, she closed her eyes, nearly overwhelmed with gratitude. He'd come. She'd dreamed of him for so long and now he truly was with her, and reality was so much better.

She kept her eyes closed as Alec carried her into his home. "We need a physician, Banks. Call one immediately," he said to the butler.

Elizabeth stiffened at the mention of a doctor. She didn't want anyone near her that she didn't know. She could feel his eyes on her and sense his worry as he swept her up the staircase, but she said nothing until he laid her on a soft bed and began to move away.

She reached for his hand. "Don't go," she whispered. "Don't l-leave me alone."

"I'll not leave, lass," he reassured her, his Scottish brogue like a welcome summer rain to her.

His mother appeared in the doorway, her hand to her mouth. "Oh, my dear girl, what has happened?" She walked into the room and came close to the bed. "Mrs. Jennings will be here momentarily with some bracing beef tea."

"Thank you." Elizabeth's throat was parched and her head ached. "M-may I have some water?"

"Of course." Isabella patted her hand. "I'll just go see what's keeping Mrs. Jennings." But before she could leave the room, Mrs. Jennings appeared in the doorway with a tray. Her gaze traveled to Elizabeth, but Isabella took the tray from her and didn't allow her into the room. "Thank you, Mrs. Jennings. That will be all."

Elizabeth was glad. She didn't want anyone to see her in such a state. Her feelings of gratitude were muddied with the humiliation of what had transpired in her household. How mortifying for Alec's mother and servants to see it and know what her father had done.

Isabella set the tray down and poured a glass of water for her. Elizabeth tried to take it, but her hand shook so badly she was afraid the water would spill out of the glass.

Alec plucked it from her and held it to her lips. "Steady, lass."

She gratefully drank every drop and lay back down. Every muscle in her body felt weak. "Thank you. I'm s-sorry to be any t-trouble."

Alec sat next to her on the bed and held her hand. "'Tis no trouble at all."

Isabella brought the bowl of beef tea to the edge of the tray. "See if you can't drink a few sips of that. You need to get your strength back."

Elizabeth wanted to please, but didn't think she could drink anything else at the moment. Isabella moved forward and touched her forehead, as if checking for fever. "I'll go get you a fresh night dress and have water sent to the chamber so you can freshen up a bit before the physician arrives."

Elizabeth nodded, too exhausted to speak.

"Let us take care of you now," Isabella said, as she withdrew.

Alec stayed at her side and he softly squeezed her hand.

"How did you know to c-come for me?" Elizabeth swallowed, her words barely above a whisper, but that was all her body could manage. She turned her head so she could see his face, blinking to bring him into focus.

"Tess came to me and told me what your father had done." Alec's voice had a thread of fury in it, and she knew it had cost him to keep his temper with her father. He was a powerful man and there was sure to be consequences for what Alec had done, but she couldn't think on that now. All she could feel was gratitude to be free. Tears threatened again as she thought of the risks Tess had taken for her.

"I feel t-terrible for Tess. H-he was so angry and grabbed her arm. He m-made her to leave and she was c-crying." Elizabeth had cried as well, knowing Tess was her only hope of being rescued. When the maid was forced from the house, Elizabeth had all but given up. She'd never felt so alone. The doctor had insisted on another "bleeding of her ill humors," and once she'd been tied to the bed, Elizabeth didn't have the physical strength to resist any longer. Then Alec had appeared.

"We'll make it right with Tess when you're feeling better," Alec said softly. "Dinna you worry about that."

She slowly reached out for his hand and pressed his palm to her face. "Thank you." Her eyes were so heavy she couldn't keep them open any longer. She felt his soft caress of her cheek before she drifted off. When she came awake again Isabella had arrived with the washing water and a fresh night dress.

As Isabella bustled around the room setting everything out, Alec moved from his position sitting next to her on the bed.

"I'll be back soon," Alec whispered in Elizabeth's ear. She felt him leave her side and listened as he told his mother that he needed to visit his solicitors and wouldn't be long, but she wasn't to open the door to anyone except the physician.

"Don't g-go," Elizabeth said, clearing her throat so she could be heard. "Please. My f-father. He'll c-come for me."

Alec was at her side immediately. "Don't be afraid. I'm taking you away, somewhere safe, *mo chride*, but I must make some arrangements before we depart." He kissed her forehead. "I won't be gone long, I promise."

Elizabeth had no strength to protest further. She lay quietly as Isabella washed her face and neck. The coolness felt so wonderful on her skin.

"Can you stand if I help you?" Isabella asked. "Then you could wash your body and we can change you into fresh clothing."

"I'm not sure." Elizabeth turned her head. She wanted to try for Isabella, but she was so weak. "Perhaps if you help me."

Isabella supported her as she rose from the bed. Draping an arm around her shoulder, Elizabeth leaned heavily on Alec's mother as they shuffled slowly to the screen. Isabella helped her out of her soiled gown that she'd been wearing for several days, and her face burned with the shame of it. Knowing what had happened, what would Isabella think of her? Of her family? She stood there in her shift, her hands hanging limply at her sides, and she swayed. She couldn't stand much longer. No matter how badly she wanted to please Isabella.

Isabella looked at her, but didn't say a word. She merely took the cloth from Elizabeth's hands and quickly finished washing her clean. Her hands were so gentle and her ministrations so much like the motherly interactions Elizabeth had always dreamed of, but never received. Tears began to roll down her cheeks. Isabella didn't make any comments, just helped her into the fresh night dress and then hugged her close. Elizabeth sank into her embrace.

"You're safe now, sweet girl. Alec and I will keep you safe." Isabella took her arm again and helped her back to bed.

"Th-thank you." Her voice was as shaky as she felt. Elizabeth lay down, her body as heavy as a brick. Her head was pounding again. She needed Alec. Wanted his touch and his soft brogue in her ear to assure her everything would be fine.

A knock sounded on the door and Elizabeth's heart rate kicked up a notch. Isabella went to the door and cracked it open, then held it wide so Mrs. Jennings could enter. "The physician is here, my lady."

An older man was in the doorway right behind her and gave her a curt nod as he moved around the housekeeper. He walked briskly to the bed. "I'm Dr. Farthingale," he said by way of introduction.

"I'm Lady Suffield," Isabella told him. "This is Lady Elizabeth."

The man bowed. "I'm told you've had quite the ordeal, my lady. May I examine you?" His voice was soft and gentle and, though Elizabeth was afraid, he seemed trustworthy.

"Yes," she agreed, "but I need her to stay." Elizabeth reached for

Isabella's hand and clasped it. Isabella stayed right by her side while he listened to her heart and lungs, He pressed on her stomach and felt her wrist for her heartbeat. He checked the bandage on her arm and replaced it with a fresh one. Isabella leaned close to hear Elizabeth's answers to the doctor's questions. All she wanted now was sleep. When the doctor finally pulled the covers over her again, she sighed in relief.

"Once the drugs have worn off, you'll just need some nourishment and rest," he told her, softly patting her hand. "You're a strong girl. I can find nothing that good food and a soft bed can't cure."

Those were the last words she heard as sleep claimed her. She could feel Isabella's presence near but couldn't keep her eyes open.

The next thing she knew, Alec was kissing the back of her hand and calling her name. "I'm right sorry to wake ye, lass, but it's time to go. Once we're in the carriage, you can sleep again."

She nodded and reached out her arms for him. He wrapped her in a quilt, then took her in his arms, and she laid her head on his broad chest. She didn't care where they were going as long as she was safe from her father and Alec was with her.

He put her in the carriage and then helped his mother to the opposite side. After taking a small item from Banks, Alec climbed in and sat beside Elizabeth. "I have some hot bricks to warm your feet," he said, holding up the package. He arranged the wrapped bricks at Elizbeth's feet and then bent to Isabella's.

The warmth from the brick was surely heaven-sent. Elizabeth could feel her body starting to relax. Alec rapped on the carriage roof, and it surged forward. Settling back in his seat, he put his arm around her, and she tucked herself into his side. Finally she could rest, both body and soul.

And she did.

CHAPTER 15

lec's arm was tingling as he cradled Elizabeth close to his chest, and even though they were close to their destination, he daren't move and wake Elizabeth just yet. To have her here and safe was the best feeling in the world. He glanced out the carriage window, breathing a sigh of relief that they were on a graveled drive. They'd finally arrived.

His mother was softly snoring, having leaned her head against the window to sleep. He was glad both women had been able to get some rest.

When the carriage eventually stopped, Alec gently squeezed Elizabeth's shoulder. "Elizabeth?"

She stirred, but didn't quite awaken. "Y-yes?"

"We're here." He shifted his arms and tucked her blankets more securely around her. The brick had gone cold hours ago and the air was as frosty as a Highland mountaintop.

She sat up and blinked at him. "Where are we?"

"Lanford Park." The footman rapped on the door before he opened it, and the sound woke his mother.

"Have we arrived, then?" she asked, straightening and patting her hair. She pulled her cloak tighter as the cold air from outside swirled around their legs.

"Yes." Alec took one more glance to make sure Elizabeth's blankets were wrapped tight. At this time of night, he didn't want to risk her catching a chill.

He alighted from the carriage first and held out his hand to help his mother down. Once she was safely on the drive, he reached for Elizabeth. He worried when he saw how shaky she was, and he could hardly resist just taking her in his arms.

"Shall I carry you, my lady?" he offered.

"If you please. My l-legs feel like jelly." She slipped her arms around his neck as if it were the most natural thing in the world and his heart skipped a beat. She trusted him and he wouldn't let her down.

He looked up at the manor house. It was everything one would expect in an earl's property, two sprawling wings with a dozen chimneys at least. Dusk had fallen and the waning rays of the sun gave it a glow, taking away some of the severeness of the gray stone and making it seem warmer. He carried Elizabeth up the front steps and met his mother who was standing in the entryway.

"Since the household staff have not yet arrived, the Lanford Park steward asked the village innkeeper's wife to kindly come and make some supper for us. Her daughter is a maid here," his mother informed him as she removed her gloves. "Apparently, your letter that we would be removing to Lanford Park was received a mere two days ago and they haven't had time to hire all the maids and footmen. I'm glad we thought to bring Mrs. Jennings, Banks, and Cook. They will be helpful in hiring the remaining staff."

A young woman came down the hall, and bobbed a curtsy when she got close. "My mum is nearly finished with your supper, and she sent me to tell you that your rooms are ready." She gaped a bit at seeing Elizabeth in his arms, but quickly hid her surprise.

"What's your name?" Alec asked.

"Betsy, my lord," she looked up at him nervously, as if expecting a reprimand.

"Betsy, would you make sure a guest room is aired? Our guest isn't feeling well and we need a place for her to rest. Please show me to the family drawing room." Alec shifted Elizabeth's weight in his arms. Her breathing had evened out again, and he knew she was still fighting the effects of the laudanum. He wanted to get her warm and comfortable as soon as possible.

"Right away, my lord." She motioned down the hall. "If you'll follow me."

She led them to a large drawing room that had a cheery fire glowing in the hearth. "I'll go and get your tray," Betsy said with another curtsy. Alec acknowledged her with a short nod, and she left the room.

Laying Elizabeth down on a long sofa that had an intricately carved back and legs, he stayed near her side, tucking in her blanket around her shoulders.

Isabella came to stand beside them. "She's going to be fine," his mother said softly. "You got to her in time."

Alec took in a deep breath. "Aye, but it was close. If we'd not gotten to her when we did . . ." he didn't want to think of the consequences. Barely leashed fury still simmered through his veins at what had been done to her, but he would deal with her father once he had assured himself she was well.

Isabella put her hand on his shoulder. "You saved her and now we'll both help her recover."

Alec brushed back a lock of Elizabeth's hair. She looked so peaceful now, but he could hardly get the image of her tied to a bed, that quack getting ready to bleed her with his leeches. "Aye, we will." He vowed it.

Betsy brought a wonderful assortment of sandwiches, fruit, cheese, and tarts. An older woman was right behind her bearing a tea tray and Alec assumed she was the innkeeper's wife. Both women set down the food and drink and curtsied. "Will there be anything else, my lord?" the older woman asked.

"We'll be retiring after we've eaten," Alec told her. "Betsy, would you please make sure there is a fire in the bedchambers?" He adjusted a pillow under Elizabeth's head. "Our guest is most unwell and we may need to call for you when she awakens."

The older woman curtsied again. "I'll help her get the rooms nice and toasty, my lord. The villagers are all abuzz to have the earl and his family in residence."

Alec gave her what he hoped was a friendly smile. "And we're happy to be here."

The maid and her mother left and Isabella made her way to the trays. She poured a cup of tea and put in the milk and sugar before bringing it to Alec. "The doctor assured me Elizabeth would be fine with rest and nourishment."

"Should we wake her to eat?" She looked so still, Alec was beginning to worry. He should have stayed to question the doctor himself, though his mother rarely forgot a detail.

"You need to keep your own strength up, or you'll be no good to her at all," his mother said, holding out the tea.

"I'm fine, Ma." He took the cup, wishing it were something stronger than tea, though he would deny himself any spirits. He needed his mind to be clear, so he could be ready to do anything Elizabeth required.

"And she'll be fine, too." Isabella returned to the tray and put a sandwich, fruit, and tart on a plate.

"Should I ask for broth to be sent up for Elizabeth?" Alec sat back, stretching his arms and legs. The carriage ride had just been long enough to make him feel as if they'd hit every bump and stone in England. He was truly grateful to be wearing a comfortable kilt instead of a cravat that could nigh strangle a traveling man.

His mother brought him food stacked high on a plate. "Eat something."

"Ye shouldn't be serving me, Ma." He lightly admonished her. "Sit yourself down, ye daft woman."

"I'm your mother, so I'm allowed to take care of you." Isabella did as he asked, however, and they both ate most of what was on the tray.

Betsy appeared in the doorway, carrying two cups. "Begging your pardon, my lord, my lady, but my mother begged me to bring this to your guest who is unwell. It is her personal remedy for settling a stomach." Alec motioned her closer and she came to his side. "It's mint tea in this cup and chicken broth in the other. I can attest that they do have healing properties."

The tea and broth both smelled wonderful. Alec took the cups from her and set them on the small table near Elizabeth's head. "Thank you for your thoughtfulness and please pass my compliments to your mother."

Betsy flushed and curtsied again before leaving.

Alec took Elizabeth's hand in his and squeezed. "Elizabeth, can ye drink something, lass?"

She opened her eyes and blinked several times, as if the room was too bright. Her eyebrows drew together. "Where am I?"

She didn't seem alarmed and Alec was glad. "You're at Lanford Park. The doctor says you need to eat. Can ye have a bit of broth or tea?"

"Tea, p-please." Her voice sounded scratchy.

Alec gently put his hand under her shoulders and helped her to a sitting position. Holding the cup, he carefully pressed it to her lips. She drank a little before pulling back. "I'm s-so tired," she told him. "So v-very tired."

"It's the drugs you were given," Isabella told her as she took the seat on the other side of Elizabeth and rubbed her back. "You might feel sleepy for a good while."

Elizabeth pressed a hand to her forehead. "I n-need to lie down."

"Of course." Alec took the teacup from her. "Your room is ready. Shall I take you there so you can sleep comfortably?"

She looked at him, exhaustion and gratitude in her eyes. "Would it t-trouble you to c-carry me there?"

"No, not at all." Alec touched her cheek, letting his thumb run over her soft skin. He'd carry her anywhere, do whatever he could for her.

Isabella rang for the maid and Alec lifted Elizabeth in his arms when Betsy appeared. She led the way to the upper floors and opened a door down the hall. "Right through here."

Alec brought Elizabeth into the room and laid her on the bed. It was an older-style canopied bed with a dark, wooden pedestal from a bygone era. The hangings smelled fresh, however, and the room was recently dusted. His servants obviously took their duty seriously. Isabella was at his side, fussing over Elizabeth's blankets and pillows. Between the two of them they managed to get Elizabeth tucked into bed.

"I'll stay with her tonight," Isabella offered. "You need to get some rest."

Alec warred within himself. He wanted to stay in case she needed him. "You need your rest, too," he pointed out.

"Why don't we take turns watching over her," his mother suggested. "I'll stay for a few hours, so you can rest. Then you can take over while I rest."

He agreed. "That sounds like a fine plan, but if she awakens and asks for me, could you have someone fetch me, please?"

"Aye." His mother's eyes were tender as she looked at him. "You did a good thing today. I'm proud of you."

He kissed her cheek. "I'm glad you're here."

Bending over the bed, he took Elizabeth's hand in his and kissed her knuckles. "I won't go far," he whispered softly. With one last glance, he went to his own room. Jenkins, his valet was there, unpacking his trunk.

"Will you need help getting out of your . . ." He looked Alec's kilt up and down, obviously unsure what to call it.. "May I help you undress?"

"Nay. You ought to find your bed. We'll address the rest of this in the morning." Alec rubbed the back of his neck. Everything would be better in the morning. He hoped.

His valet left and Alec slowly took his *sgian dubh* and laid it on a table near the fire. Taking off his hose, kilt, and buckle, he laid them on the bed and stood there dressed only in his shirt. The clothing represented such a large part of him, and staring at them, it occurred to him that he'd been trying to put aside so much of what he'd known as a Scot to become part of English society. He wasn't going to do that anymore. He was going to wear a kilt if it pleased him. He'd speak with his brogue.

And anyone who didn't like it could go hang.

Aye, he was an English earl, but he was also a Highlander. He'd been taught in the ways of the brave Highland warriors who had gone before him, and he wouldn't disgrace their memory by tucking that heritage away like an old boot with no more use in it. Nay, he would do his best to combine both worlds in his life, and he hoped a certain young lady would want to be part of that future.

And he would do his best to convince her.

CHAPTER 16

*E*lizabeth could hear the low rumble of voices and opened her eyes. She was in a brightly colored room decorated with greens and yellows. Definitely not her bedchamber at home. She turned her head and saw Alec and his mother. They'd stopped talking and noticed she was awake.

Alec reached her first. He sat down in the chair close to the bed and took her hand in his. "How are you feeling?"

"Better." And she did. The horrible, sleepy feeling was gone and her head wasn't hurting. Only her arm still throbbed. "How l-long have I b-been asleep?"

"Two days. I admit, I was starting to worry." His thumb caressed the back of her hand and warm tingles flowed up her arm.

"I never knew my son to be such a worrier. He's hardly left your side and pesters me often about your condition and what we can do for you." She smiled and moved to the upper side of the bed so Elizabeth could see her, since Alec's broad shoulders took up so much space. "You must be hungry."

"Quite th-thirsty, actually." Elizabeth swallowed. Her mouth felt as if it were stuffed with cotton.

"I can fix that." Isabella turned and walked to a pitcher on a table near the window.

Alec watched his mother for a moment, then turned to Elizabeth. He kept his voice low, though this mother would have to be hard of hearing to miss his words in a nearly silent room. "I'm glad to see you awake, lass. I've missed the sparkle in your eyes." He smiled down at her and Elizabeth could see the relief in his eyes.

She shook her head at his compliment, however. "I must l-look a sight."

"A beautiful sight." Alec could hardly take his eyes off her and a flush crept up Elizabeth's neck. Did he truly think her beautiful? It seemed so hard to believe, but he'd never lied to her before. The thought of his regard made her blush deeper.

Alec's attention was diverted when Isabella handed him the glass of water. "Will you hold this while I help her sit up a little more?"

He let go of her hand to take the water and Elizabeth missed the warmth of his hand immediately. But she dutifully leaned forward while Isabella arranged the pillows. "Th-thank you," she murmured.

After she'd had a drink, she sank back into the pillows. She felt as weak as a newborn kitten, but her mind was clear and she felt stronger than she had the day before. That was a bit of progress. She closed her eyes for a moment. She would have to be patient. Getting her strength back would be a lot of small steps that she hoped would eventually lead to her full recovery.

"Alec, why don't you go down and tell Cook that Lady Elizabeth is ready to break her fast?" His mother gave him The Look that every mother is an expert at---the one that communicated silently to her child exactly what she wanted them to do.

He inclined his head, getting her meaning right away: he needed to give the ladies some privacy. Elizabeth blushed, sure he'd guessed that she needed to use the necessary. How embarrassing, but there was nothing she could say that would ease the awkwardness, so she stayed silent.

"Of course," he replied, ever the gentleman. She was grateful he didn't make any other comment, merely squeezed Elizabeth's hand. "I'll be right back."

Elizabeth wanted him to stay, but she also wanted to use some of the time she had to make herself presentable. At least use the tooth powder and find a brush for her hair. Isabella must have sensed her need and held up a brush from the dressing table. It was so strange to be fussed over by someone other than a maid, but a small part of her soul had longed for that sense of love and belonging. She had found that with Alec and Isabella, and she didn't want to lose it. Ever.

She watched Alec leave, admiring his broad shoulders and trim waist, then, turning, she saw Isabella's eyes on her, her mouth in a wide smile.

"He's as handsome as his father was," Isabella said with a wink. "I can tell you're feeling better, my lady, and it does my heart good to see it. Can I help you wash and put on a fresh night dress?" Isabella offered. "I'm sure it would help lift your spirits even more." She glanced at the closed door, then gave Elizabeth a sly smile.

Elizabeth pressed her lips together, suppressing a laugh. Isabella was far too observant. "It definitely w-would." And maybe she'd even put a ribbon in her hair to help her feel as beautiful as Alec already thought she was.

ONCE HE'D GAINED the hall, Alec went down to the kitchens. Cook, Mrs. Jennings, and Banks had all arrived late last night. He was grateful his mother had insisted on bringing the London servants until they were more sure of the situation at Lanford Park. It had been a brilliant idea, especially now that they were aware that Lanford Park had only been working with a skeleton staff. Thankfully, Betsy's mother was all too happy to let Cook take over her temporary duties. She hadn't minded filling in for a while, but she had four children at home to care for and had only been coming to the estate to make sure things were in order. Alec had asked to keep Betsy on, and her mother had agreed.

Cook pressed the back of her hand to her brow before continuing to punch down some bread dough. She looked up when Alec came through the door. "My lord, you shouldn't be down here," she scolded. "The earl calls for his servants to come to him, not the other way around."

He gave her his most charming smile. He was coming to like his English servants. "I've come to snitch some shortbread. I can't resist ye, ye ken."

"Oh go on with you," she laughed.

"Truth be told, my mother sent me to say that Lady Elizabeth has awakened and is needing to break her fast." Alec walked around the table and spied a plate of tarts cooling on the windowsill. Glancing back, he took one and popped it into his mouth.

"I saw that." Cook's back was turned, but Alec had no doubt he'd been caught.

"I canna resist your baked goods," Alec said after he'd swallowed his ill-gotten gains.

"You go back and tell your mother a tray will be sent up shortly." Cook smiled as she continued to knead the dough. "We'll have Lady Elizabeth right as rain in no time."

Alec hoped so. Now that she'd awakened and seemed to be coming back to her old self, it was as if he could breathe again. He made his way back upstairs and found Kitty in the hallway with a footman.

"I'll take her to my mother," Alec volunteered. And perhaps Elizabeth wouldn't mind a wee visitor as well. He took the dog carefully in his arms and knocked on the door.

"Come in," his mother called.

Alec walked into the room and his gaze immediately went to Elizabeth. She was sitting up in bed, her hair brushed and tied back with a ribbon and she had his mother's blue dressing gown on. She looked as beautiful as the first day he'd seen her.

"I found a visitor waiting outside your door, my lady," he said, petting Kitty's head.

Kitty nearly jumped from his arms the moment he came close to the bed. Elizabeth laughed and wiggled her fingers. The little dog went to her side and lay down as if she'd been waiting for the opportunity. Elizabeth patted her head. "There's a good girl." Kitty gazed up at her with an adoring look.

"Kitty is quite fickle with her attentions, wouldn't you say, Ma?" He moved to his mother's side.

Isabella looked at the pair on the bed with an amused smile. "She obviously has made a friend."

Betsy arrived with a tray laden nearly to the edge with toasted bread, marmalade, eggs, ham, and honey cake. The delicious smells made Alec's mouth water as well. He was reminded that he hadn't broken his own fast yet, beyond a stolen tart, and would wager his mother hadn't, either.

"Oh, I'll n-never be able to eat all of this," Elizabeth exclaimed. "Won't you join me?" She looked between Alec and his mother.

"Let me help you make a plate," Isabella said, moving to her bedside. Isabella smoothed the bedcovers and put a little of everything on a plate for Elizabeth. Alec could see how much his mother enjoyed being needed and it warmed his heart to see the woman he loved getting along so well with her.

Alec moved two chairs over and they all sat to eat their meal together. Breaking his fast in a lady's bedchamber was an unusual arrangement, but an enjoyable one. Being with Elizabeth was a joy and the rapport between the three of them was comfortable. He watched Elizabeth laugh as she tried to keep Kitty away from the ham, but then finally gave in and fed her little morsels.

"She's d-delightful," Elizabeth said with a grin. "I started sketching her when I was . . . l-locked in my r-room." Her voice trailed off and her eyes dropped to the coverlet.

"Would you like to talk about it?" Alec asked softly. He wanted to hear more details, but only if she was ready to share.

She let out a small sigh. "My f-father locked me in my r-room until I agreed to m-marry Lord Lindley. I r-resolved to stay strong, and when I hadn't changed my m-mind after a few d-days, my father was f-furious." She looked up. "He c-called that h-horrible doctor." Her voice was so quiet, now Alec had to lean forward to hear. His jaw was clenched so hard he was sure his teeth would be ground to powder at any moment.

"I-I tried to r-resist," she whispered.

Her lips were trembling and Alec took her hand, stroking her delicate fingers. "*Wheest*, now, lass, you're safe here with us. We won't let anything happen to you."

Isabella handed Elizabeth a handkerchief. "I wish I could have seen your father's face when Alec carried you off."

One side of Elizabeth's mouth quirked up as if she daren't fully smile, but found a bit of humor in the situation. "It was a frighteningly spectacular sight. I don't think I've ever s-seen his face so red. I thought he might have an apoplexy on the spot." She picked at the stitching on the coverlet. "Do you think he will f-find me here?"

"Nay, lass. All the servants have been warned not to let him in and to inform us at once if they see any sign of him." Alec squeezed her hand. "Dinna fash yourself over it." He wanted her to focus on her recovery. He would worry about her protection.

Her fingers moved over his, and she squeezed his hand. Her touch speared his heart with warmth. "Th-thank you," she said softly.

Isabella leaned in as well, making the moment feel very much like a family gathering. "I wanted to tell you that I know you weren't able to bring any clothing with you since you weren't planning on traveling, but I brought the ones I'd recently had made at Madame Villiers. They haven't been worn, and we're of a similar size, so I hope you'll accept them. Though they aren't the style for a young woman like yourself, I think they will do until you can have some other gowns delivered."

Elizabeth's jaw went slack. "My lady, that's such a generous g-gift. How can I ever r-repay you? Both of you." She reached out her hands and Alec and Isabella each took one. "How did I get so l-lucky to have both of you as my guardian angels?"

Alec cleared his throat. Could she not see how he felt about her? "Och, lass, 'tis I who am the lucky one." He stood and bent to gently kiss her on the forehead. "You might not see me as a guardian angel when I have to remind you to stay abed. But I will offer you a boon. Shall I go down to the library and find a book to read to you? If you can stand my Scottish burr that is."

"I love your burr." She yawned. "I am a little t-tired, so reading would be j-just the thing. Poetry, perhaps?" She lay back against the pillows, her contented smile enough to soothe Alec's heart. She was going to be just fine.

And he would do all in his power to make sure she stayed that way.

CHAPTER 17

*E*lizabeth was restless. She'd spent the last two days in her room and though Alec had done his best to entertain her with poetry and listening to his excited plans for his thorough-bred, Ares, she was ready to go downstairs, or walk in the garden. She needed to see something other than the four walls surrounding her. Betsy knocked and at her invitation, came in with a tray.

"I'd like to get dressed in a day gown," Elizabeth told the girl. "Would you help me?" Even making the request made Elizabeth miss Tess. Hopefully, once her circumstances were more stable, she could find her and ask her to come back as her lady's maid.

Betsy curtsied. "Of course, my lady." Going to the wardrobe, Betsy looked at the available dresses that Isabella had hung there. "What about this pretty pink one?"

Elizabeth nodded. The dress had a little lace at the bodice and was understated, yet flattering. "Yes, that will do nicely."

Once she was dressed and had put her hair up in a simple chignon, Elizabeth moved to the door. Perhaps she would surprise

Alec in the drawing room. Or the library. From the way he'd been choosing books and reading to her every day during her recovery, she'd wager that was where she would likely find him.

"Could you help me find the library?" she asked the maid, before she left the room.

Betsy agreed, and the women walked slowly down the main staircase. Elizabeth took in the portraits that hung on the walls of past earls and countesses of Suffield. Alec had some similar features in the shape of his eyes and nose, but he definitely had a unique look. No one could dispute that he was his own man.

They turned past the staircase and walked down a long hall. Elizabeth was beginning to tire a bit but persisted. She wasn't ready to return to her bedchamber yet. When she'd finally arrived at the library and Betsy had left her, Elizabeth wandered to the shelves and perused the titles. It was a beautiful room with enough books in it that it could rival Hatchard's. Turning a corner, she pulled back, startled. "Oh!"

Alec reached for her elbow. "What are you doing out of bed, lass?" His voice wasn't angry, merely concerned. She gave him her most brilliant smile, hoping to convince him to let her stay downstairs.

"I needed a change of scenery." She touched his arm as his brows drew together and he began to shake his head. He was going to send her back to bed. "Please don't be upset. I haven't overtaxed myself. I need to be up and moving."

He led her to a small settee and helped her sit, then sat down next to her. "Och, I'm not upset with ye. In fact, I was just coming to look for ye. We must have a wee talk."

Elizabeth noticed a missive in his hand, and her stomach tightened with dread. "Has something happened?"

"Aye." His eyes were solemn. "Christian has written to say that your father is whispering in some important ears that you aren't in full possession of all your faculties, and I've deceived you and spirited you away. He wants you back and will use any means necessary to do it."

Elizabeth gasped. "What will he do? Is he coming here?"

Alec touched her shoulder. "I don't think he knows where we are. He seems to be trying to find out, but he definitely wants you committed to the asylum. If he can have you declared incompetent, he can sign the papers that would leave you to their care."

Elizabeth's hands flew to her mouth. She couldn't go to an asylum. Just being under that doctor's care for three days had given her nightmares that she was still struggling with. "What c-can we do?"

"Your options are limited, but you do have some available." He took her hand in his and leaned in. She gazed at him, his green eyes steady and sure. "You can run away. I will help you hide and leave no trace of where you've gone. It would be no trouble to set up a trust with money for you that your father could never find. But you'll be looking over your shoulders for months or even years, depending on who your father hires to find you."

His thumb was caressing her knuckles and making those warm tingles shoot up her arm at the movement. "And the others?" Looking over her shoulder in fear for weeks or months didn't appeal in the least.

He sighed and ran his other hand through his hair. "Aye, there's one other option." His look was so intense she felt pinned to her spot. "You could marry me."

The words echoed in the room. Had she heard him correctly? "You would do that for me?" Her voice was small. She cared for Alec and was fast falling in love with him, but she didn't want him to marry her out of obligation.

Alec pulled back, watching her carefully. "I would do anything to keep you out of such an asylum," he said. "Every time I think of what you've already been through, I wish I'd been able to plant a facer on your father that he wouldn't soon forget."

Elizabeth put a hand to her middle. "So you would marry me to keep me away from my father." Not because he loved her. Her stomach sank like a boulder thrown into the Thames. She'd merely fooled herself that he felt more than merely friendship or possibly pity for her. Why would he want someone like her?

Alec glanced her way, then, as if reading her thoughts, took both her hands in his. "Elizabeth." He stopped and cleared his throat. "If ye had the protection of my name, your father would never get near you again if ye didna wish it. But I don't want to force you into marriage like your father was trying to do. You should be able to make your own choices and I never want you to resent me."

Her shoulders relaxed a little at his words. Was that what he was worried about? "Oh, Alec. You wouldn't be f-forcing me, but I d-don't want to be more of a b-burden to you. Look at everything you've already been through because of m-me." She couldn't meet his eyes. "What if *you* c-came to resent *me*?"

Alec's hand slid up her arms and he moved scandalously close. "Elizabeth, you could never be a burden to me. It would be my privilege and honor to have you for my wife. I-I care deeply for you, lass. And I swear by all the Saints that I would do my best to see you happy for the rest of your days if you married me."

Elizabeth's heart was pounding so hard she felt light-headed with it. He cared for her. He wanted her for his wife. She leaned forward slightly, until her lips were only a breath away from his. This was her chance to have everything she'd ever dreamed of---a man she could respect and the potential to have a marriage full of love and laughter. "Yes."

Alec's hand moved to the nape of her neck and a shiver of delight went down her spine as he caressed that sensitive skin.

"You'll marry me?" His voice was low and heat seemed to shoot through her veins at the sound of it.

"Yes," she repeated.

His green eyes darkened and he closed the distance between them, capturing her lips and pressing her to him. She slid her arms around his neck as they sealed their promise with a kiss. Elizabeth was breathless when he drew back, and her hand slid to his chest, feeling his heartbeat galloping as fast as hers was.

"Are you thinking of t-taking me to Gretna Green?" she asked, trying to distract herself from wanting to pull his head down to kiss him again.

Alec grinned. "Nay. Your father might try to dispute a hasty marriage, and I want something better for you than an anvil wedding. Before I spirited you away, I went to the Doctors Commons, and with the help of the Marquess of Wolverton and using the Duke of Argyll's connection to the Earl of Suffield, I was able to purchase a special license." He reached inside his coat pocket and drew forward a parchment.

"You were so s-sure of me?" she teased, letting her hand brush over his jaw. The stubble was rough on her palm, unlike anything she'd ever felt before. He was a mystery she was going to enjoy unraveling in so many ways.

"I wanted to be prepared," he answered, pushing a loose curl behind her ear. "And I'm right glad I was."

She laid her head on his heart. "I am, too."

"I know we're not really doing things in the traditional fashion, but there is one Scottish tradition I'd like to observe." He shifted underneath her and pulled something out of his pocket. Taking a breath, he held up a small brooch. "I'd like to give ye something for our betrothal, short though it may be."

Elizabeth straightened and looked at the piece of jewelry that looked so delicate in his large hand. "Alec, it's b-beautiful." The silver brooch was of two intertwined hearts with an emerald in the middle of them.

"It's a luckenbooth brooch," he said, his thumb running over it. "It's been in my family for generations. A man offers it to his betrothed to protect her from the evil eye, and then the wife pins it on their newborn's blankets to protect the babe from the fairies." He shifted to face her more fully. "The intertwined hearts symbolize love, and the emerald is said to symbolize truth and hope for a marriage and family. I want to give this to you, *mo chridhe*. I want to have this with you."

Elizabeth's eyes pricked with tears at his declaration. "This is the most l-lovely gift I've ever r-received." And it was. No one had ever given her a gift so wondrous. "B-but I have nothing for you."

He took the brooch and carefully pinned it to her gown. "*You are my gift, lass.*"

She looked down at the brooch over her heart, then touched her palm to his chest. Her love for him surged through her and she closed her eyes at the overwhelming emotion.

He tipped her face and kissed her gently on the mouth before he pulled back to a proper distance. "We'd best go find my mother and inform her there's to be a wedding here tomorrow morning."

Elizabeth laughed, her heart lighter than she could ever remember it being as he pulled her to her feet. "Do you think she'll be s-surprised?"

Alec's eyes twinkled. "Nay."

Elizabeth slipped her arm through his and tucked herself close to him. Tomorrow she would be married.

And God willing, there would be no surprises to mar the day.

CHAPTER 18

*A*lec had dismissed his valet, wanting to dress for his wedding by himself. His kilt with the Campbell colors made him wish that more of his family would be attending his nuptials today, especially his Uncle Colin. But it couldn't be helped.

A knock sounded at the door and he turned. "Enter."

His mother bustled in and stopped when she saw him. "You look very handsome," she said, coming to stand in front of him and brushing a hand over his right shoulder. "Your father would be so proud."

"I wish he were here. Or Uncle Colin." Alec looked down at his mother. "But I'm very glad that you're with me today."

His mother's eyes were shining, and she pressed her lips together. "Don't make me cry now." She dabbed at the corner of her eyes with her fingertips. "Everyone we love will be with you in spirit."

"I know, but it's good to hear you say it." He looked down at her hand that was clutching a small bouquet. "What do you have there?"

"I went and picked some wildflowers this morning and put in a bit of white heather that I'd brought with me from Scotland." She smiled up at him. "It's dried, but I reckon that luck will still follow it."

"I'm sure Elizabeth will be pleased. We might need a wee bit of extra luck. Even if it's to be found in Scottish heather." He kissed his mother's cheek. "Thank you."

"I was just on my way to give it to Elizabeth, but wanted to stop in your chamber and impart a few thoughts." His mother took his hand and drew him to a chair near the hearth. She sat down, and he took the matching chair near it.

"What did you want to say?" he asked. She seemed a wee bit nervous, which wasn't like her.

"I know you don't have many memories of your father, but one thing he always said was that he wanted you to be free to marry for love. I know that your marriage to Elizabeth is unexpected, but do you love her?" His mother watched him intently.

Alec took a breath, wanting to say it out loud to someone. He'd been holding it in for weeks, mulling it over in his mind, afraid he couldn't have her and would always love her from afar, but today, he would marry her. She would be his. "Aye, I do."

Isabella smiled. "I believe she loves you, too. The way her eyes follow you, and the connection you two have had from the very beginning . . . well, I think the Fates have watched over you both."

"I want to earn her love, but until we've settled this situation with her father, we won't be able to move forward as a couple." He ran his palms down his kilt. "I did want to speak to you about something myself, Ma."

"Oh?" Her eyebrows raised expectantly.

"I've been doing some thinking, and I know you wanted me to

fit in, but I find that I can't squeeze into the role London society would have me play. I'm a proud Scot as well as a new English earl. I want to do the best I can to represent all that's good and noble from both countries, but I don't want to forfeit either identity. I want to blend them, and find my way with each." He exhaled and looked into his mother's eyes, hoping he didn't see disappointment there. "Do you ken what I mean?"

"Aye. I was wrong to ask you to try to change at all. I've made a wonderful friend with the Duchess of Huntingdon. And I believe you have a rapport with the Marquess of Wolverton. Even if they are our only friends, I would be satisfied." She stood and kissed his forehead. "You're wise beyond your years, my son."

"So, you're not upset? We may not have society's regard when we return to London after what's happened with Elizabeh. Combined with our Scottish heritage, we might have a difficult time of it." Alec had thought she would try to convince him to try once again to conform to British expectations. She had agreed so easily.

"You and Elizabeth are what's important now. I'm not upset at all." She patted his forearm to reassure him, then held up the small bouquet. "I must go if you're going to have any luck for your wedding today."

"Don't let me keep you." He took a deep breath as she closed the door behind her. He checked his pocketwatch. It was almost time.

He made his way downstairs to the drawing room, and when he entered, he grinned. He'd sent an urgent message late last night to Christian and he'd obviously gotten it. Both he and Alice were standing near the window, talking to the vicar. They must have traveled all night. They turned at his arrival and he strode over to them. "Elizabeth will be so happy to see you both. I'm so glad you made it."

Christian shook his hand. "We were afraid we would be too late. Thank you for your invitation."

Alice stepped forward, searching his face. "How is she?"

"She seems recovered from her ordeal." Alec clenched his hands. "She suffered greatly at her father's hand, however."

"That's partly what I came to talk to you about," Christian said. "I don't want to bear ill tidings, but we should speak after the ceremony."

Alec wanted to know exactly what Christian's information was, but Elizabeth was about to come down and he would want her to hear anything Christian had to say. He would set everything aside until later that had to do with the duke. "We'll talk in the study after the wedding breakfast, then." He motioned behind him. "I'd be honored if you and Alice would be our witnesses."

"We would be delighted." Christian and Alice took their positions near the window. If they'd traveled there that morning, they'd been on the road for hours, yet they both looked fresh and alert. He'd have to ask them what road they'd taken, for the one he'd driven on to get to Lanford Park had been so bumpy he'd wondered if there was a smooth patch of more than a mile between here and London.

He turned to the vicar and greeted him. "A fine day for a wedding," he said to the clergyman, who quickly agreed.

Isabella appeared in the drawing room doorway and smiled brightly. "The bride is here so we can begin."

She stepped forward and Elizabeth came into view. She was wearing a deep-sapphire blue gown that made her complexion glow. The white lace at the sleeves drew his eye, and he saw his luckenbooth pinned over her heart. *She wore it.* His heart swelled with pride at all she'd endured and overcome. She was an extraordinary woman.

Elizabeth moved into the room, her eyes on Alec, but when she saw the two witnesses, she audibly gasped and tears formed in her eyes. Brushing them away, she walked toward them and hugged Alice. "How did you know I was getting married today?"

"Alec sent a message last night and I'm so grateful he did." Alice hugged her again. "I missed you so at my own wedding; I'm so very glad I can share yours."

Elizabeth was beaming as she turned to Alec. "Now everything is perfect."

He walked toward her and took her hand. She carried the wildflower-and-heather bouquet in her other hand, the dried heather peeking out from the middle. Seeing the Scottish good luck charm and the brooch on her person, Alec silently agreed. Everything was perfect.

But they still had one more guest to make a grand entrance. Alec watched with amusement as Kitty walked in wearing a flower wreath around her neck. Her little doggie face looked as happy as it could, as if she was secretly pleased with her matchmaking success. Isabella called to the dog, and they both sat on the front row of chairs.

Alec drew Elizabeth close to his side, and they faced the vicar. He felt the warmth of her hand through her glove, and awareness flared through him. They were about to become man and wife. He glanced over at her as she listened to the vicar's words on the sanctity of marriage. She was so beautiful. The morning sun gilded her hair, making it appear as shiny as a new sovereign coin.

He couldn't pull his gaze away. She was his treasure, more dear to him than any amount of coin. Though, once things were settled, he wanted to talk to his solicitors about setting aside some funds into a trust, with a stipulation that Elizabeth be able to use the funds when and how she wished. It was one more way to show her that he trusted her to make her own choices---that love wasn't a restriction on her freedoms.

She turned to him with a question in her eyes. She motioned toward the vicar, as if she knew he hadn't been listening. He lifted a shoulder in a half-shrug. How could he focus on words with her standing next to him? He couldn't believe what a lucky man he was.

Minutes later, after he'd repeated his vows and Elizabeth had given hers, and the minister had finally pronounced them man and wife, Alec took Elizabeth's hands in his and faced her. "*Mo chridhe,*" he whispered for her ears alone.

He cupped her cheek, gently tipping her chin so he could claim his wife's kiss. Wonder stole over him, and he paused to commit the details to memory. Her blue eyes sparkled as she quirked an eyebrow at the delay. Kitty barked as if to tell him to *hurry up*, and Alice, Christian, and his mother laughed, but Alec was only aware of Elizabeth, anything else paling in comparison to this moment with her. She put her hand over his and he drank in her smile before he lowered his mouth to hers with a kiss that promised fierce love, loyalty, and a lifetime of happiness.

His mother's clapping brought him back to the present, and he slowly drew away. The dazed look on Elizabeth's face was exactly how he was feeling inside. He took Elizabeth's hand and turned where they were hugged and congratulated.

Isabella ushered them toward the dining room. "Cook has prepared a very special wedding breakfast that is not to be missed. It will be unforgettable, really," she promised.

Alec seated his wife to his right and his mother on his left, with Alice and Christian next to Elizabeth. It was a cozy group, and no one could stop smiling. When the newly hired footmen brought in the food, Alec's smile grew even wider.

"Haggis with neeps and tatties. My favorite dish in all the world: Cranachan. Have I died and gone to heaven?" he asked, looking at the traditional Scottish food. He turned to his mother. "Did you know this was on the menu?"

"I made the menu with Cook's blessing." Isabella said, shrugging one shoulder. "It seemed only right, and Cook was happy to try to bring some of your favorite foods to the wedding table."

"Aye." More food was being brought out, plates of sausage, ham, coddled eggs, kippers and the like, but Alec only had eyes for the Scottish food. He'd missed it so.

Elizabeth touched his hand. "Will you l-leave any for the rest of us?" she teased, tilting her head toward the haggis.

"I might not," he said, slipping off her glove so he could touch her skin. She was his wife now. He had the privilege of being called her husband. His heart beat a little harder at the thought, and he lifted her hand to his lips and kissed the back of it. He'd not felt this much happiness in many a year.

Once they'd eaten their fill, Christian stood and motioned to Alec. "Would you like to retire to your study? We have much to discuss."

Elizabeth looked between the two men. "What's wr-wrong?"

"Christian wants to discuss some things regarding our situation." Alec kissed her cheek. "I wanted to wait until you could be there to hear what he has to say."

"Thank you. I should l-like to be there." Elizabeth squared her shoulders. "I'd like to know what is being s-said and done."

"So many men don't think women should be included. I'm glad to see your husband is a forward-thinker," Alice said, smiling at Alec. "Christian is always grateful to have my thoughts and ideas."

Christian looked at Alice and quirked an eyebrow. "Your thoughts and ideas are almost always beneficial to me, dear wife."

"*Almost* always?" she teased. "I'll have to remind you of this conversation in the future when my ideas have helped you solve a complex problem."

Christian took her hand and kissed the back of it. "Please do."

She laughed and looped her arm through his. "Oh, believe me, I will."

Alec observed the love between the two of them. He'd have his own chance at that sort of intimacy and love with Elizabeth now that they were married. The time would come when she would smile and laugh at something he'd said, and they would have jests between them that only they would understand. He could hardly wait.

He wiped his mouth with his serviette. The haggis had been nearly as good as the ones he'd regularly consumed in Scotland. His stomach was definitely in charity with the world, but at the mention of Elizabeth's father, the contented feeling had soured somewhat. "Would you excuse us, Ma? We shouldn't be long."

"That's quite all right. With all the excitement this morning, Kitty and I will just go have a lie-down." She bent to pick up her little dog. "Please keep me informed of any developments."

"I certainly will." Alec led the way into the hall and down to his study. Once they'd entered and the ladies were seated on the chairs in front of the large oak desk, Alec sat down at the chair behind it. Christian remained standing, though he leaned against the hearth.

"I'll get right to the point," Christian said, making eye contact with each person in the room. "A magistrate is coming to visit Lanford Park in the morning at the behest of the duke. There's to be an inquiry into Elizabeth's mental state."

Elizabeth gasped, but said nothing.

Christian continued. "I've been trying to understand what is driving the duke to go to such lengths and to find out what the bargain was that he struck with Lindley's father. But so far, I can't find any details on either issue. Do either of you have any ideas?" he asked as he looked from Alec to Elizabeth.

"I c-can't think of any reason at all." Elizabeth folded her hands in her lap. "He seemed almost d-desperate for me to m-marry Lindley right away, but he n-never shared his reasons with me. I assumed he was anxious to be r-rid of me."

Alec hadn't had many interactions with the duke, and none of them had been positive. But something tickled at the back of his mind. "When I was at the Veterans Club, there was a man there who knew the duke. Called him a coward and said he was surprised that someone as good as Elizabeth had come from such a selfish man."

Elizabeth frowned, her eyebrows drawn down. "That's strange. Are you sure he c-called my f-father a coward?"

"Did your father serve in the military, then?" Christian asked.

"Yes. He was a m-major in the army and s-served during the war in the Americas. He never spoke of that time to m-me." Elizabeth's eyes met Alec's. "Perhaps that veteran s-served with him."

Alec's mind was racing. If the man had served with the duke and had information on possible cowardly conduct, perhaps they could gain the upper hand on the duke, or at least have something to leverage over him. "We need to find that veteran as soon as possible."

"With the magistrate coming here tomorrow, we'd best go back to London tonight and try to find him." Christian looked at Alice. "I would suggest that Alec and I go so that we can travel light, but what are your thoughts on the matter, my dear?"

"I think we should all go," she said with a nod. "Then we can be at your side when this matter is resolved."

Alec leaned his elbows on the desk. "Perhaps my mother can tell the magistrate we've been recently wed and are on our wedding trip. That would seem a plausible excuse, and then we can concentrate on finding out just what your father is hiding."

"He doesn't see m-me as whole." Elizabeth cleared her throat and met Alec's gaze. "Perhaps he just w-wants me out of his s-sight."

Alec crossed his arms over his chest. The hurt her father had heaped upon her went deep, but her inner strength and the love of her new family with Alec and Isabella would get her through. "There's something afoot here that's more than that," he said. "And we're going to find out what it is."

She gave him a small smile and stood. "I'd better go pack a trunk, then."

"I will, too," Alice agreed, rising from her seat.

Alec came around the desk and escorted Elizabeth through the door and into the hallway. He gave her a quick kiss. "Are you happy, wife?" he asked, looking down into her sweet face.

"Y-yes. Are you?" She tilted her chin up and he was sorely tempted to kiss her for longer than would be proper while they stood in the entryway.

"I've never been so happy." He couldn't resist and touched his lips to hers, reluctantly drawing away.

She wrapped her arms around his neck. "I'm glad to hear it." She stood on tiptoe and kissed him once more. "But if we're to leave soon, I r-really must pack."

He watched her go up the stairs, knowing deep in his bones he would never tire of being with Elizabeth. She had completely entranced him.

The only thing left to do was to make sure she was out of her father's reach.

For good.

CHAPTER 19

*E*lizabeth was nervous as they approached the doors of the Veterans Club. They'd reached Suffield House just as the sun was beginning to rise that morning. She'd made sure to draw the carriage curtains as they passed her father's home. Even the thought of seeing him now made her stomach queasy. Exhaustion was starting to seep into all the muscles of her body, but she had to see this through.

Alec drew her hand through his arm and made sure she was securely fitted to his side as they waited to be admitted. He always seemed to know when she needed a bit of extra courage and was happy to provide it. Reams opened the door to the club, and Alec and Elizabeth had followed Christian and Alice up the stairs.

They checked each salon, but didn't find the man Alec had talked to until they peeked in the last reading room before the dining area. He was asleep in an overstuffed chair. He had a long beard that could use a trim, and deep lines etched into his face that attested to a harsh life. The man looked so comfortable Elizabeth briefly considered letting him snore on, but she needed answers.

Christian gently shook the old man's shoulder, and he opened his eyes and stared at them for a moment, before he quickly stood and saluted. "Yes, Captain?"

"Please, sit." Christian motioned for him to take his seat again and the ladies sat down as well. Alec stood behind Elizabeth's chair.

"What's your name?" Christian asked.

"Percy Barstow." Though he sat, Percy's back was stick-straight.

"I'm told you know the Duke of Barrington," Christian put his hands behind his back, looking every inch the captain he'd once been.

The old man bit his lip and stared at Christian as if trying to gauge what information he was being asked for. "Yes, I knew him. I know what he did."

Elizabeth took a breath, trying to prepare herself for what she was about to hear. Her father was such a private man and image mattered to him. She'd never heard anyone speak ill of him before, but she wanted the truth.

"What did he do?" Christian prompted.

Percy pressed his lips together and was silent, as if weighing his options. Lifting his chin, he began to speak. "Course he wasn't the duke then. He was merely a viscount and a major in the army. My brother was his second-in-command when he was in the American colonies fighting them rebels. They'd received orders to march to Fort Chambly to help protect it from attack, but when the company marched through a small valley, enemy forces opened fire from all sides. The major and his men barely had a chance to draw their weapons. Nearly all of them were killed."

Elizabeth could hardly fathom it. Her father had commanded men on a battlefield? "How did my father s-survive?"

"His horse was shot out from under him and landed on the major, trapping him. Lucky his only injury was a broken leg, but when the enemy discovered he wasn't dead, they surrounded him and boasted about how they would take turns running him through." The old man rubbed a hand across his grizzled beard.

Elizabeth could hardly sit still. "What h-happened then?"

Percy raised his eyes to hers and she saw sorrow, anger, and accusation shadowed in their depths. "He offered to show the rebels how to take the fort from British hands in exchange for his release. Gave them the layout of the fort and everything else they'd need in regard to men and provisions and the best time to attack."

"That's treason." Alec's words were clipped and they echoed through Elizabeth's head. Her father was a traitor.

"Yes, it is." The man looked at Alec. "He's a coward and a traitor. He thought no one knew of his actions, that he could return home and forget it ever happened. But I know what happened." He thumped his chest. "We were marching behind the duke's men and came upon the scene. My brother was yet alive, but barely. He told me what happened before he took his last breath."

"Why did you not say something?" Christian asked softly.

"I made a report, but nothing came of it. The old duke most likely protected his traitor son and buried it all. Besides, who would believe the son of a blacksmith over a major in the King's Army and son of a duke? But when Fort Chambly was easily taken by the Continentals, I knew who was to blame." He spit on the floor. "That duke didn't care about anyone but himself. My brother lay in the dirt for hours, dying, while his commanding officer didn't have to answer for his actions and left his men to rot. I'll never forgive him for that, begging your pardon, my lady. You seem a good sort."

Elizabeth inclined her head, still shocked by what she'd heard. "Th-thank you." She couldn't think of anything else to say.

"Would you be willing to swear out a statement?" Christian asked Percy.

"Why would I need to do that?" Percy looked suspicious. "It was a long time ago."

"We're trying to save someone else from the duke's maltreatment. He believes himself above the law, and it's time he found out that he isn't." Christian tilted his head toward Percy and leveled his gaze at him. "You may be the only person who can help us and avenge your brother's death."

Percy's face brightened at Christian's words. "In that case, I'll do it." He brushed his hand over his stained shirt. "I'd like to help my brother finally be at rest."

Christian turned to Alec. "I'd say a visit to the duke is in order. Now that you have information that would constitute a hanging offense against him, perhaps you can make him see it's in his best interest to leave Elizabeth alone."

Alec immediately agreed. "I'll take Elizabeth to Suffield House and then you can meet me at the duke's residence with the statement."

Elizabeth shook her head. She'd been afraid for too long, and it was time to face her fears. "I'm c-coming with you."

Alec went to her side and crouched. "*Mo chridhe*, I cannot risk your safety. Please, you must stay at Suffield House while I attend to your father. He's unpredictable at the moment, and searching for you. A magistrate is most likely at Lanford Park as we speak, hoping to interview you on your father's behalf."

Elizabeth looked into his dear face. She had to make him understand. "My f-father has never listened to me. He's p-pushed me aside. He's t-trying to have me c-committed to an asylum. I need my chance to speak to him and h-have him hear every word." Surely Alec could understand that.

He took in a quick breath. "I will take you on one condition. That you stay by my side every second we are in that house."

"I promise." She wouldn't want to be anywhere else. Her father was thoughtless and cruel, but this time, they had the upper hand. "What w-will you s-say to him?"

"I want him to retract every untrue statement he's made about you, then leave England and never return. For what he's done, that punishment is a mercy. He should be hanged as a traitor to the Crown." Alec's voice was firm and confident. It gave her a bit more courage, too.

"He'll not g-go quietly," she warned.

"He won't have a choice," Alec said grimly.

"I'll meet you at the duke's as soon as I have Percy's statement," Christian said, but amended his statement when he caught Alice's eye. "*We'll* meet you at the duke's."

Elizabeth and Alec took their leave. It was a silent walk back to the carriage, each lost in their own thoughts. Alec helped her into the carriage and then sat beside her. "How are you holding up, lass? I know that probably came as a shock to you."

She leaned her head on his shoulder. "My f-father is a s-selfish man. Though I am surprised that he would commit treason, I know he would do anything to s-save himself." She softly sighed. "I see now, it's not that my f-father didn't l-love me. He was incapable of l-loving anyone but himself." As strange as it seemed, the thought was comforting. It wasn't her failing or anything she'd said or not been able to say. Her father just wasn't able to love her.

"Aye, and I'm glad that you know it." He gently turned her head and bent to kiss her. "But you won't be without love ever again, *mo chridhe.*"

His lips were soft against hers, and she clung to him, wanting to make the world outside disappear until there wasn't anything left beyond her and Alec. "What does *mo chridhe* mean?" she asked softly when they drew apart.

"My heart. And ye captured mine the moment I saw you, lass." He put her hand on his chest, directly over his heartbeat, then covered it with his fingers. "Ye steal my breath with your smile, and I crave your company." He kissed her knuckles. "I love you."

She leaned in, happiness filling her heart. "I love you, t-too." She slipped her hands out of his grasp and placed her palms on both cheeks. "How fitting that the carriage is nearly in the same spot I was standing when I rescued Kitty that first day."

He chuckled and pressed her to him. "Ah, lass, I wish we didn't have such a sorry business to attend to, that we could be starting our marriage on a happy note, with only sweet memories. But it can't be helped." He met her eyes. "You remember your promise, now. Stay close to me. I'll not have you hurt."

She nodded. Her heart pounded so hard she felt a little light-headed. This was her chance to face her father.

They walked up the stairs, and when their butler, Cartwright, opened the door, his eyes widened to see her. Alec handed him his card. "The Earl and Countess of Suffield request an audience with the duke."

Jenkins silently took the card and motioned for them to enter. "Please wait in the parlor."

Elizabeth didn't reply, merely turned to the doorway to the family's formal receiving parlor. She didn't sit, but instead looked at the place she'd called home for so long. None of it evoked any feeling in her. Living here felt like a lifetime ago. She hadn't felt accepted or loved in this home. Not as she had in just the few days she'd been in company with Isabella and Alec. They'd become her family and showed her what that word could truly mean.

Her father entered the room with her mother trailing after him. She didn't meet Elizabeth's eyes, but the duke sneered when he saw them. Elizabeth's hand tightened on Alec's arm.

"Come to flaunt your disgraceful behavior to my face, have you? Sullying the family name by marrying this Scot?" The duke waved at Alec.

Elizabeth's tongue suddenly seemed too big for her mouth, as it always did in her father's presence. She swallowed hard and took a breath to calm herself. "N-nothing I've done has s-sullied the family name. Perhaps you r-refer to your t-treasonous acts."

Her father scowled. "I can barely understand a word you're saying. What are you blathering on about, girl?"

"She's speaking about a witness statement that you traded sensitive information to the enemy for your life during your war service." Alec's voice was calm, but his muscles were tense. He was watching her father carefully.

The duke paled. "I would never." His tone was belligerent. "How dare you come here and accuse me of such a thing!"

"We're going to do more than accuse you. With a sworn state-ment, we can have you brought up on charges in the House of Lords. You may well be hanged." Alec's tone was harsh and he stared at her father, pinning him with his gaze. "Seems a fitting punishment to me after all you've done to your daughter."

"All I've done to her?" Her father's face was turning red. "I've given her my name, let her live in my home even with a pronounced malady, and found a man to marry her in spite of it." His voice was rising with each sentence. "And all she had to do was wed that whelp Lindley, and the family honor would stay intact."

"Lindley's father knows what happened while you were in the army, doesn't he?" Alec's tone was steady, even in the face of her father's rising agitation.

"Yes, he knows." The duke threw up his hands with a growl and began to pace. When he stepped too close to Elizabeth, Alec straightened, his stance protective and ready. She squeezed his arm, grateful he was here.

"He wanted to recommend me for a medal of valor. Thought I should be recognized for my service. But he came across an old report that my father was told had been burned." The duke glared at Elizabeth. "I don't owe you any explanations, but I barely escaped alive. I tried to get out of that infernal wilderness to tell someone what had transpired before the fort was taken. But I was sick with fever and worried I'd never walk again. I did what I could."

"You could have h-held your t-tongue in the f-first place," Elizabeth told him, her chin held high. "You've g-given *me* that advice m-many times."

"Don't speak to me in that tone, young lady." His father pointed his finger at her. "I am your father."

"You are my t-tormentor," she countered. "You've n-never been a father."

He raised both palms and shook his head. "What would you have had me do? Lindley's father offered his silence about my past actions if you agreed to marry his son. Lindley would have your dowry for their empty family coffers, and I would write an addendum to the settlements to give his father an annual sum as well. In exchange, he would stay quiet, and the Barrington family name would remain above reproach."

"The f-family name has n-never been above reproach b-because of what you did that d-day in the Americas." Elizabeth straightened her back.

"What do you know of it, you dim-witted girl? I almost died. And when my company didn't arrive for reinforcements, the rebels would have taken that fort anyway." The duke balled his hands into fists. "My actions just hastened the inevitable is all."

Elizabeth's mother stood and faced her husband. "So you admit this accusation of treason is true? And you're trying to justify it?"

"Shut up, Eleanor." The duke turned away from her. "You're like an annoying bee always buzzing in my ear."

Her mother flew at him. Her slap on his cheek rang out through the room. The duke grabbed her hands and shook her.

Hard. "Don't you ever touch me," he said, his face pinched in fury.

"I wouldn't want to," her mother said, tears rolling down her face. "I've done nothing but my duty as your wife. I bore you children. Went against my better instincts, telling myself you knew best in trying to find a situation for our daughter that would benefit us all. But no more. You don't deserve loyalty, and you never did."

"Unhand her," Alec commanded. "Now."

The duke pushed past her and strode angrily to Elizabeth. Alec tensed and moved slightly in front of her. "Do you see what you've done? If you'd just obeyed me, we all could have gone on and lived happy lives."

"Except m-me." Elizabeth said softly. She looked at the man who had sired her and felt nothing put pity. "I wouldn't have b-been happy with Lindley, but you d-didn't care. You w-wanted what was b-best for you."

"You ruined everything," he hissed. He reached into his pocket and pulled out a small pistol, pointing it at Elizabeth. "All you had to do was marry him. I thought if your only other alternative was the asylum, you would obey. I *needed* you to obey! I worked too hard for years to lose everything now!"

The gun shook in his hand, and Elizabeth tried to put some distance between her and Alec. If her father was going to shoot her, she didn't want him to hit her husband. Alec's hold was like an iron band, however, and didn't allow for any space between them.

Elizabeth's mother appeared at her side and stepped between Elizabeth and the duke. "You'll never hurt our daughter again." She grabbed for the gun, and her father was caught by surprise and thrown off balance. They struggled and fell to the floor. Before Alec or Elizabeth could intervene, the gun went off.

Elizabeth's ears were ringing, and she covered them with her hands. Servants rushed in with Christian and Alice close behind. The duke was on the floor with a chest wound, bleeding onto the Aubusson rug, and her mother was lying next to him, sobbing, blood spattered all over her best blue silk.

Alec pulled her hands from her ears, holding them in his. His eyes were worried as he looked into her face. "Are you well?"

She could only stare at him, knowing just beyond her husband's broad shoulders that were blocking her view, was a blood-covered scene she'd never be able to forget.

Alec gathered her in and held her close. "It's all right now. It's going to be all right."

Christian had taken charge and was barking orders to the servants, but he wasn't calling for a physician. Elizabeth had known when she looked at the duke that he was dead, but even thinking that was strange to her mind. Her father was dead.

Alice helped Eleanor to the sofa and put an afghan around her shoulders. Alec led Elizabeth to sit beside her. Though she'd never been close to her mother, they clung to each other now. Her mother's tears were coming in great, gulping sobs and Elizabeth could only pat her back in a small attempt at comfort.

"I'm sorry," she said in Elizabeth's ear. "So very sorry."

Elizabeth rested her head on her mother's shoulder, turning away from the men putting a sheet over her father's body. Even with all that had happened, so was she.

CHAPTER 20

The week following the duke's death was chaotic, but Alec was amazed at the strength of his wife. The inquiry into the circumstances surrounding what happened that morning was exhausting, but she bore every interview and question with her head held high. Whenever he was near, Alec used every chance he had to touch her hand, shoulder, or the small of her back to let her know he was there should she need him.

Often, after the last visitor had left Suffield House and her mother had retired to bed, Elizabeth would shut the door to the parlor and join him on the sofa. He would rub her neck and shoulders, ply her with tea and cakes, and then they would sit quietly watching the fire, enjoying the momentary privacy. Everyone in London seemed to be talking about the scandal from the members of the ton to the lowliest servants---the questions and judgmental whispers following them whenever they left the house. Alec saw firsthand what his mother had meant about rumors in the ton and how it could affect a person.

Alec did his best to shield both Elizabeth and her mother, but the gossiping tabbies were everywhere, and they all wanted the latest on dit. The only recourse was to closet themselves at Suffield House until after the funeral. They limited visitors to only Christian and Alice, but even their friends agreed that it might be best to retire to the country. So, the moment the funeral was over, Alec gave their direction to the dozens of solicitors that were dealing with the ducal estate affairs, then he took the women back to Lanford Park to recover from the shock of it all.

His mother and Mrs. Jennings clucked and fussed over them from the moment they arrived. Alec sat in the parlor with the ladies and read poetry, built up fires, and made sure food was brought at regular intervals. He'd begun riding in the mornings with Elizabeth, greeting the sunrise from a small knoll on the edge of Lanford Park property. Those rides were one of the few times Elizabeth seemed to relax and let herself smile and he cherished those moments with her. She'd confided that she was at peace with her father's passing and more concerned for her mother than anything else. Her words made him hopeful for a fresh, new beginning for all of them without specters from the past shadowing their steps.

Her mother, Eleanor, spent a lot of time in her room at Lanford Park. Isabella and Elizabeth sat with her every afternoon. The women had talked and talked, then talked some more. His mother told him that sometimes talking was the best way to work through trouble and that's what Eleanor was trying to do. Elizabeth had seemed comforted by their conversations, but he could tell she cried sometimes. Alec held her close when she needed it, and though he wanted to press to know what they talked about, he let her grieve at her own pace. They were all muddling through.

After a week at Lanford Park, the cold seemed to have a bigger bite to it. Autumn was quickly turning to winter and reminded Alec of the mountain air surrounding his Highland home just before the snow flies. No matter how chilly it was outside, however, Elizabeth still took a walk in the gardens after teatime. He searched her out that afternoon and found her on a bench in the corner of the garden, her sketchbook in hand. She was looking down at a drawing, her brows knit together.

He spotted his luckenbooth pinned to her gown and the sight spread a feeling of contentment through him. They belonged together. Their hearts were as intertwined as that brooch she wore. Sometimes it was difficult to fathom how he'd won Elizabeth's heart, but he was glad he had.

"What masterpiece have you created today?" he asked as he approached her.

She looked up when he spoke, and her lips curved into a small smile. "How d-did you know?" She tilted the drawing so he could see what it was.

"May I?" He reached for the paper. It was a detailed picture of him, dressed in his shirt, kilt, hose, and sporran, the way he'd worn them on their wedding day. He could hardly believe how she had captured his expression, down to the look of love in his eyes. "Lass, it's wonderful."

"Do you r-really think so?" She put a finger to her chin and looked at the drawing. "I wasn't sure if it needed a b-bit more shading r-right here."

She pointed to a small corner of his kilt, but Alec shook his head. "Nay, it's perfect just as it is. I can't wait to show off your talents to my clan in Scotland."

"Or is it your p-portrait you want to show off?" she asked with a laugh.

"Maybe a bit of both," he admitted with a grin. "But it's the best gift I've ever received." He leaned over and pressed a light kiss to her mouth. "Thank ye."

She let her hand linger on his arm before she took the drawing from him and set it on her sketchbook. "My m-mother is leaving t-today."

Alec put his arm around her shoulders. "That's a surprise." Was she sad about that? He couldn't tell.

"One of my f-father's solicitors s-stopped by this afternoon and showed her the m-marriage settlements. Apparently, her d-dowry included a small c-cottage on the coast, but the d-duke thought it beneath him, so she had no idea and has n-never been there. The solicitor said it's in g-good repair, and it's one place that is f-free of any difficult memories." Elizabeth's eye clouded over for a moment. "She wants to b-begin again. I think we all do."

Alec squeezed her shoulder. "Aye. Starting fresh can be wonderful, yet daunting. But, if you like, perhaps we can visit once she's settled. And after we're settled, too, of course."

She stared at the barren garden in front of her. "Yes, p-perhaps after we're s-settled."

Alec reached for her hand to pull her back from her woolgathering. He'd wanted to show her something, and now seemed like the perfect moment. "Will you come inside with me?"

Elizabeth looked at the sky, where the sun was valiantly trying to shine through the clouds. "A f-fire and a w-warm cup of tea might be nice. I think my f-feet are turning numb with how c-cold it's gotten."

"Hot tea and holding you in my arms before a warm fire, would be just the thing," he raised both eyebrows in question and she dipped her head in agreement, a blush pinkening her cheeks. "But after I show you my surprise," he finished.

Alec gathered her pencils and sketchbook, then tucked her arm in his elbow as they strolled back to the manor.

"I like s-surprises," she said, shyly.

She looked up at him so tenderly, his heart nearly expanded out of his chest. He wanted to make every one of her wishes come true.

Putting his hand over hers and pulling her closer to his side, he relished having her near. "Will your mother leave George here with you? I think he will go into a decline if she doesn't. Your dog has become quite attached to Kitty. Those two are inseparable now."

Elizabeth laughed. "Yes, if you d-don't mind another d-dog in the family. George is loyal and the b-best of friends. He's obviously w-won over Kitty."

"Your friends, canine or human, are always welcome here." Alec led her to the terrace doors that led into the library. Once they were inside, he put her drawing materials on a table, then shut the door tight again before he took her hand. "Almost there."

"Where are we g-going?" she said, her blue eyes sparkling with delight.

"You'll see soon enough." He drew her into a darkened room but let go of her hand to cross the length of it and open the drapes. Afternoon sunshine lit the room, and Elizabeth walked toward him, her skirts swishing on the polished floor.

"Why are we in the b-ballroom?" she asked as she slipped her arms around his waist.

"I seem to remember a beautiful woman telling me once that she dreamed of freedom and wanted to shout at the sky after a bruising ride." He raised his eyebrows. "At the time, I offered her the next best thing." He pointed to the paintings that covered the ceiling. "I suggested we shout at poor wee bairns in the clouds." He kissed the top of her head. "Do you recall?"

"Aye, I d-do recall mentioning that." She looked up at the ceiling, then quickly looked down, pressing her face into the front of his jacket. Her shoulders began to shake. Was she crying?

Alarmed, he held her away from him. Her face was red and her lips pinched together, but Elizabeth wasn't crying. She was trying not to laugh and losing the battle.

"I can't shout at the wee b-bairns. It wouldn't be m-mannerly," she managed to say between giggles. "I think the b-bairns are supposed to be a r-rendering of Cupid. A s-symbol of love. Have you never seen one? A p-proper one?"

Looking down into her face wreathed in smiles, all he could feel was his love for her. "Och, if all of those bairns are a symbol of love, no matter how badly they're painted, then this might become my favorite room in the house." He brushed a curl from her neck. "I love you, *mo chridhe*, and I always will."

He pulled her to him, their breaths mingling for just a moment before their lips met. Time seemed to stop as her hands slid around his neck. She was everything his heart had longed for and been waiting to find his entire life.

And he couldn't wait to spend that life with her.

Julie Coulter Bellon is an award-winning author of nearly two dozen published books. Her book The Marquess Meets His Match won a five star review from Readers' Favorite, All Fall Down won the RONE award for Best Suspense, Pocket Full of Posies won a RONE Honorable Mention for Best Suspense and The Captain was a RONE award finalist for Best Suspense. Most recently her books, The Capture and Second Look were both Whitney finalists for Best Suspense/Mystery.

Julie loves to travel and her favorite cities she's visited so far are probably Athens, Paris, Ottawa, and London. In her free time, she loves to read, write, teach, watch Hawaii Five-O, and eat Canadian chocolate. Not necessarily in that order.

If you'd like to be the first to hear about Julie's new projects and receive a free book, you can sign up to be part of her VIP group on her website www.juliebellon.com

facebook.com/AuthorJulieCoulterBellon
twitter.com/juliebellon
instagram.com/AuthorJulieCoulterBellon

Made in the USA
Middletown, DE
23 July 2021